PRAISE FOR THE J

THR

"In Robinson's latest action f Team--a Delta Forces unit whose gonzo members names of chess pieces--tackles his most harrowing mission yet. Threshold elevates Robinson to the highest tier of over-the-top action authors and it delivers beyond the expectations even of his fans. The next Chess Team adventure cannot come fast enough."-- **Booklist - Starred Review**

"In Robinson's wildly inventive third Chess Team adventure (after Instinct), the U.S. president, Tom Duncan, joins the team in mortal combat against an unlikely but irresistible gang of enemies, including "regenerating capybara, Hydras, Neanderthals, [and] giant rock monsters." ...Video game on a page? Absolutely. Fast, furious unabashed fun? You bet." -- **Publishers Weekly**

"Jeremy Robinson's *Threshold* is one hell of a thriller, wildly imaginative and diabolical, which combines ancient legends and modern science into a non-stop action ride that will keep you turning the pages until the wee hours. Relentlessly gripping from start to finish, don't turn your back on this book!" -- **Douglas Preston, New York Times bestselling author of Impact and Blasphemy**

"With *Threshold* Jeremy Robinson goes pedal to the metal into very dark territory. Fast-paced, action-packed and wonderfully creepy! Highly recommended!" -- **Jonathan Maberry,** *New York Times* **bestselling author of** *The King of Plagues* **and** *Rot & Ruin*

"*Threshold* is a blisteringly original tale that blends the thriller and horror genres in a smooth and satisfying hybrid mix. With his new entry in the Jack Sigler series, Jeremy Robinson plants his feet firmly on territory blazed by David Morrell and James Rollins. The perfect blend of mysticism and monsters, both human and otherwise, make *Threshold* as groundbreaking as it is riveting." -- **Jon Land**, *New York Times* **bestselling author of** *Strong Enough to Die*

"Jeremy Robinson is the next James Rollins."-- **Chris Kuzneski, New York Times bestselling author of The Lost Throne and The Prophecy**

"Jeremy Robinson's *Threshold* sets a blistering pace from the very first page and never lets up. This globe-trotting thrill ride challenges its well-crafted heroes with ancient mysteries, fantastic creatures, and epic action sequences. For readers seeking a fun rip-roaring adventure, look no further."
-- **Boyd Morrison, bestselling author of** *The Ark*

"Robinson artfully weaves the modern day military with ancient history like no one else."-- **Dead Robot Society**

"THRESHOLD is absolutely gripping. A truly unique story mixed in with creatures and legendary figures of mythology, technology and more fast-paced action than a Jerry Bruckheimer movie. If you want fast-paced: you got it. If you want action: you got it. If you want mystery: you got it, and if you want intrigue, well, you get the idea. In short, I $@#!$% loved this one."-- **thenovelblog.com**

"As always the Chess Team is over the top of the stratosphere, but anyone who relishes an action urban fantasy thriller that combines science and mythology will want to join them for the exhilarating Pulse pumping ride."-- **Genre Go Round Reviews**

CALLSIGN:

KING

BLACKOUT

JEREMY ROBINSON

WITH SEAN ELLIS

BREAKNECK MEDIA

Visit Jeremy Robinson on the World Wide Web at:
 www.jeremyrobinsononline.com

Visit Sean Ellis on the World Wide Web at:
seanellisthrillers.webs.com

FICTION BY JEREMY ROBINSON

SecondWorld

The Jack Sigler Thrillers
Threshold
Instinct
Pulse

Callsign: King – Book 1
Callsign: King – Book 2 - Underworld
Callsign: Queen – Book 1
Callsign: Rook – Book 1
Callsign: Bishop – Book 1
Callsign: Knight – Book 1

The Antarktos Saga
The Last Hunter – Descent
The Last Hunter – Pursuit
The Last Hunter – Ascent

Origins Editions (first five novels)
Kronos
Antarktos Rising
Beneath
Raising the Past
The Didymus Contingency

Writing as Jeremy Bishop
Torment
The Sentinel

Humor
The Zombie's Way (Ike Onsoomyu)
The Ninja's Path (Kutyuso Deep)

FICTION BY SEAN ELLIS

The Nick Kismet adventures
The Shroud of Heaven
Into the Black
The Devil You Know

The Adventures of Dodge Dalton
In the Shadow of Falcon's Wings
At the Outpost of Fate
On the High Road to Oblivion (forthcoming)

Dark Trinity: Ascendant

Magic Mirror

Secret Agent X
The Sea Wraiths
Masterpiece of Vengeance
The Scar

CALLSIGN: KING

BLACKOUT

PROLOGUE—DEMON

The Kushan Empire, 250 CE

Vima gazed out at the assembled group—the entire population of the village had turned out to watch him confront the demon—and felt a surge of apprehension. His fear was not for his own life but rather for theirs.

He recognized nearly every face in the assembly. He had broken bread with many of them, particularly since his victory in the games, where he had demonstrated that he was indeed the strongest and bravest of all the warriors in the district. There was no higher honor than to have the chosen one dine at your table, and in the days since the games, he had eaten well. More importantly, he had made friends of people who had previously been only strangers with familiar faces.

His fear was for their safety. The *magi* had made it very clear to him that if he somehow failed in his task, if *Angra Mainyu* was displeased with the offering he was to leave upon the evil one's very doorstep, then he would be only the first to die. Every man, woman and child gathered here to observe would also surely perish.

Vima felt the hands of the *magi* and their acolytes upon

him, prodding and tugging him, and allowed himself to be
maneuvered to the front of the throng where the chief *magus*
waited with the sacrificial animal. A low murmur rippled
through the crowd, and though Vima could not make out the
words, he knew what was being said; it was as if the entire
village possessed a single, unified mind.

God has deserted us. Ahura Mazda, *the personification of
light and wisdom has abandoned his creation to the appetites of
chaos.*

Vima felt it too. He had heard the revelations of the ancient prophet Zoroaster all his life, but attaining a deep
understanding of the mysteries of the universe had never been a
priority for him. Nevertheless, he knew enough to recognize
that making an offering to appease *Angra Mainyu*, the source of
all darkness, ought to have been unthinkable. *Angra Mainyu*,
the demon of chaos and madness, was the enemy of all *Ahura
Mazda*'s creations. Vima knew that in some lands people wor-
shipped many deities, some of whom embodied dark forces, but
such was not the way of his ancestors. That the *magi*, the priests
who kept the revealed wisdom of the prophet, had proposed
making such a sacrifice was ominous indeed.

Vima had heard also of a new religion spreading across the
land like a fire in late summer. This faith, it was said, held that
there was no God at all, but that the universe and all within it
were part of an endless cycle of life, death and rebirth. Many
were embracing this new belief, leaving aside the religions of
their ancestors. Perhaps the widespread growing disbelief was
the very reason *Ahura Mazda* had abandoned them to the
appetites of his enemy.

Vima didn't know if there really was a God, or many gods
as some believed, but the demon was most assuredly real. Of
that, he was certain.

The *magus* thrust a length of rope into Vima's hand, then
raised his arms and spoke an invocation before the assembled

crowd. Vima barely heard the desperately hypocritical prayer; no one here believed this act was God's will, and no one believed that salvation would come from that source.

The prayer concluded and Vima felt the hands of the *magi* prodding him once more into motion. He gathered his courage and took a step out into the open area where the demon's presence was a tangible reality.

There was no mistaking the zone of the demon's influence—a rough half-circle, more than a hundred paces across, where the ground had been scoured down to bare rock by the entity's appetite. When the demon had first become manifest, only six months earlier, the affected area was only a few paces across, but with each passing day, the demon's hunger increased and the dead area grew.

After only a few steps, Vima felt the rope in his hands go taut. He glanced back and saw the sacrificial animal, a goat, stubbornly refusing to move. He gave the rope a sharp tug and managed to drag the beast forward, but it continued to resist, planting its hooves squarely on the rocky ground and pushing back with all its might. With a snarl of frustration, Vima reversed course, thrust one arm under the goat's belly, and lifted it off the ground as he might a wayward child.

Even as he moved, he was acutely aware of the demon's influence. The air felt thick and moving through it was more like swimming than walking. Yet, when he drew the goat up to his chest, the resistance vanished and he almost stumbled backward into the blighted area. The goat struggled in his embrace and for a moment; it was all he could do to stay on his feet.

A murmur arose from the crowd, but Vima quickly discerned that the disturbance was not related to his difficulties. Rather, the attention of the group was focused on a new arrival, a runner from one of the sentry outposts, bearing urgent news. Vima purposefully ignored this new development and focused all his attention on accomplishing the task at hand. He turned with deliberate care, feeling the inexorable attraction of the demon's hunger, and faced his goal.

The demon's cave was a blank spot on the face of the sandstone cliff. Unlike the other caves and depressions that pitted the sheer rock surface, the void was no mere place of deep shadow where the sun's rays did not reach. *Angra Mainyu* consumed light just as he consumed everything else, and so looking into his domain was like staring into a hole in the fabric of reality. Vima tore his gaze away from the nothingness, looking instead at the ground directly in front of him, and took a cautious step forward.

Although the ground beneath his feet was flat, he felt as if he was descending a hillside; walking required no exertion at all, and the idea of breaking into a run was strangely seductive. Through a conscientious effort, he resisted the impulse, leaning back, away from the demon's tempting presence, and slowed his pace even as the sensation intensified with each step forward.

When he reached a point almost exactly halfway between the assembled villagers and the cave, the demon's powerful attraction was almost too strong to resist. Walking normally was impossible; with every step, he felt as though he might pitch forward, or be snatched off the ground and sucked into the demon's maw. He turned his body sideways, perpendicular to the cave opening, scooting his feet along the rocky terrain, one leg extended and locked to brace himself against the dark entity's hunger. After moving ahead a few more paces, he realized that continuing forward would spell certain doom.

Close enough, he thought, preparing to heave the squirming goat in the direction of the cave.

"No!"

The shout from behind him sounded strange, like something from a dream, and in that moment, Vima realized just how quiet the world had become. Aside from the frantic bleating of the sacrificial animal, he hadn't heard a sound for what seemed an eternity. Curious, he turned to locate the source of the shout and discovered a stranger venturing into the blighted area behind him. The man was tall and broad, and he was clad in a robe of saffron-colored cloth. His olive-skinned visage, framed by a mop of curly hair and a thick beard to match, marked him as a foreign visitor to the land of the Kushans. He was cautiously moving toward Vima, waving his arms with exaggerated slowness and repeating the shouted negative. Vima's gaze slipped past the approaching stranger and fell upon the gathered crowd of his fellow villagers. They had been joined by a group of men—likewise wearing bright yellow robes, but with shaved heads and facial features more common to inhabitants of the region. Strangely, both the newcomers and the villagers were completely motionless. Vima stared at them for a moment, expecting one of them to move, but the tableau did not change; the men and women were as still as statues.

With astonishing suddenness, the curly-haired stranger reached the place where Vima was standing. His momentum nearly caused a collision, and as Vima recoiled instinctively, he felt the goat slip from his arms.

The animal landed awkwardly and even as it struggled to get to its feet, it began tumbling forward, drawn in by the demon's irresistible hunger. Vima had half-expected this to happen, but he could not have anticipated what the stranger did next. To Vima's complete surprise, the big man threw himself onto the rope trailing behind the goat and caught it in his massive hands. He had time to wrap a twist of the line around his wrist before it went taut, snapping rigid as if connected to a team of chariot horses. The stranger's jaw clenched and the muscles of his upper arms bulged as he began straining to haul the goat back from the demon's maw.

Vima managed to overcome his shock. "What are you doing? You must not interfere with the sacrifice."

Mindful of the invisible force that had snatched the goat,

he took a tentative step forward and knelt alongside the stranger, attempting to wrestle the rope from the man's grasp. The hands that held it were as unyielding as forged iron. Nevertheless, the stranger snarled at him, and then said something in a language that Vima did not recognize.

Vima redoubled his efforts. The man might have been as strong as a water buffalo, but Vima had proven himself in games of skill and combat, and he was no trifling opponent. Besides, he did not need to overpower the stranger; all he had to do was get the man's grip on the rope to weaken.

He tried striking the man with a closed fist, but his arms now felt as heavy as lead. The man shrugged off the ineffectual blow and then, with the casual indifference of someone shooing away a fly, let go of the rope with his left hand and wrapped his fingers around Vima's throat.

Dark spots clouded the young warrior's vision and all thoughts of doing his duty and delivering the sacrifice were pushed aside by an overwhelming desire for self-preservation. His hands went to his throat, struggling to loosen the iron grip but his strength fled along with his grasp on consciousness.

The stranglehold did relax, but not because of anything Vima had done. At the edge of complete darkness, he felt the man release him and then, with no more effort than that required to pick up a sleeping child, the big man tucked him under one arm.

Vima was faintly aware that the man had begun to move, crawling along the ground and dragging his twin burdens. Vima felt heavy, as if mired in mud, but as the man pulled him further from the demon's cave, the sensation diminished. When they had crossed about half the distance to the assembled group—the crowd was no longer statue still, but their movements seemed unnaturally slow and languid—the big man got to his feet and quickened his step. Vima's head cleared enough to make another attempt at resisting his captor, but the man seemed to sense his intention and tightened his grip, keeping Vima all but completely immobilized. Then he spoke. "Do not fight. I am trying to save you."

The words were delivered haltingly, giving evidence of the foreign man's unfamiliarity with the language. "You will destroy us all," Vima countered, the words burning past the ache in his throat. "If we do not feed the demon—"

"If you feed this thing, its hunger will only grow greater." The man offered no further explanation, but a few moments later, they reached the assembled villagers who were now moving normally. The *magi* were talking animatedly with the yellow-robed monks, but then the big man spoke loudly in a language Vima did not comprehend. All conversation ceased and every eye turned toward him.

"The darkness in the cave cannot be appeased with offerings," one of the monks translated. "It will only grow stronger and consume everything: the village, the mountain, the entire world."

Vima struggled to his feet, ready to engage the man in combat if so directed, but judging by the rapt expressions of the priests, it was evident that his own role in the drama had ended. The *magi* craved guidance; God had abandoned them and the decision to make an offering to the demon had been one of desperation, not divine inspiration.

"What can we do?" implored the chief *magus*.

A grim but satisfied smile turned up the corners of the big stranger's mouth as he spoke again.

"The darkness that threatens you is the embodiment of desire. Desire, hunger, greed...these things can be conquered through meditation. I will teach you a mantra—"

The monk did not translate this word, but Vima inferred that it must be something like a magic spell.

"—in the language of the first people," continued the stranger. "When you chant this word, together in one harmonious voice, and empty your minds of all desire, the darkness will depart. Will you do this?"

The *magi* exchanged a glance and then the chief *magus* addressed the foreigner. "It may be that God has sent you. We will do this."

The next few moments were surreal, like something from a dream. Vima had been prepared to offer his life, if necessary, to end the demon peril, but this was almost beyond his comprehension. With the rest of his fellow villagers, he surrendered completely to the guidance of the monks, and sat down on the rocky ground at the edge of the area that had been scraped raw by the demon's hunger. In a matter of only a few minutes, they were arranged along the semicircle, and all were, like Vima, looking to the stranger for direction.

The monks, stationed at equidistant points around the perimeter, translated the man's stentorian utterances. "The mantra I will teach you is but a single word. You may know this word, for it is a word of great power and many who seek truth by different paths have discovered it. All of the universe is contained in this word, and when you say it, you will become one with the cosmos."

There was a pause and then the men in saffron robes began to hum in unison, a single syllable. "Om."

Vima shivered as the sound resonated in his chest. The utterance lasted only for a few seconds, then ceased at a gesture from the stranger.

"When the monks raise their arms, you must breathe in deeply, filling your lungs with air. Imagine that your body is a clay pot, and that you are pouring air into it, filling it up slowly, from the bottom to the top."

The monks proceeded to raise their arms, and Vima heard a rushing sound as the entire population of the village inhaled together. To his surprise, he also began to draw in air, caught up in the power of the foreigner's charismatic presence.

"When they lower their arms, you must sound the mantra until your breath is no more. Then breathe and utter the mantra again." The stranger let his gaze sweep across the gathering. "Once we begin the mantra, the word must continue to be spoken without interruption. No matter what happens. Only in this way can the darkness be conquered."

Just when Vima felt his lungs were about to burst, the monks lowered their arms and the villagers began to hum. Their combined voice was low and discordant at first, as if some were uncertain about committing to this strategy. Vima certainly was; he was a warrior, and his faith was in the strength of his hands and his skill with arms, not in magic chants invoking foreign gods. And yet, what had he accomplished with his might and prowess? He had not even been able to best the foreigner, much less defeat the demon.

Banishing his doubts, he closed his eyes and focused on the mantra, channeling his breath into the back of his throat, letting the sound reverberate against the roof of his mouth and out through his nose. The other villagers also seemed to have set aside their reservations, for by the time Vima was forced to draw another breath, the air had come alive with a steady and insistent hum.

The mantra vibrated through every fiber of his being and distorted his perception of time...of reality itself. Hours might have slipped by or perhaps only a few minutes, but his awareness of the world was reduced to that single syllable, his ability to reckon the passage of time measured only by uncounted discrete inhalations.

But then something intruded on his strange calm. A disharmonious vibration shuddered up from the ground beneath him like a note played by a *setar* with a loose string. Vima's eyes fluttered open and he heard the intensity of the collective humming diminish as his fellow villagers became distracted by the strange tremor.

"Keep uttering the mantra!"

The stranger's words, translated and repeated by the monks, wove into the fabric of their chant, gently but insistently guiding them back, yet even as Vima closed his eyes again, the hostile vibration intensified. It was not merely a discordant false note, but a shaking that arose from the earth itself.

An earthquake, Vima realized. A groaning noise, as of mill-stones grinding together, filled the air, drowning out the sound of the diminishing hum.

"The darkness resists you," the stranger said. "If you falter, it will consume you. No matter what happens, keep saying the word!"

Vima felt the truth of the exhortation. He had stood upon the threshold of the demon's cave and knew its terrible hunger. It seemed impossible that they could conquer it with nothing more than a foreign word—a single syllable—yet the very fact that it was now fighting them was proof of the efficacy of the mantra. But would it be enough?

Vima realized that it was too late for that question. The battle had been joined and there could be no retreat. Closing his eyes again, he willed himself to ignore the violent tremor and focused only on his breath.

Fill my lungs as I would a clay pot... Utter the mantra...

"Om..."

Suddenly, the ground heaved and Vima was thrown into the air like so much chaff. Even as he slammed back down, a deafening thunderclap tore through the air.

The combined hum of the villagers quieted still more, and cries of alarm began to shoot through the droning mantra. More thunderclaps and tremors followed, building to a crescen-do, but through it all, the voice of the stranger kept guiding them back. "No matter what happens..."

Fill the pot with air... "Om..."

The sound of the mantra, welling up from within and joined by dozens of voices from all around, persisted and enfolded Vima in a blanket of calm, even as the earth seemed to shake itself apart.

For a long time, the opposing forces vied for dominance, like objects being weighed in a scale, but as the initial shock of the demon's counterattack began to subside, more and more voices returned to the chorus. The grinding noise of the earthquake diminished into nothingness as the air began to vibrate once more to the sound of that single ancient and potent word.

Vima was not conscious of the moment when the struggle ended. Like the transition between wakefulness and sleep, it happened with imperceptible subtlety. He did not notice the abrupt end of the tremor or the final crushing sound of boulders dislodged in the quake settling into place. It was only when the stranger spoke again—loudly and in the language of the Kushans—that Vima realized they had won.

"It is finished."

Vima's eyes fluttered open and he let the mantra slip away into a sigh. The air around him was thick with settling dust, but through the pall, Vima could see that something had changed. The area that had once been scoured clean by the demon's appetite was shot through with gaping cracks and littered with loose rocks, but the most dramatic difference was the cave itself. No longer was there evidence of the surreal nothingness, the hole in reality, which had marked the demon's presence.

Angra Mainyu was gone.

A low wail began to issue from the villagers, cries from those who had suffered minor injuries during the quake and complaints from some who could, even from a distance, see that their homes had been knocked flat, but Vima paid no heed.

"We did it!" he cried, turning to the stranger. "We have defeated the demon."

The foreign man gave a heavy sigh. "A darkness like this can never be truly defeated. It only slumbers. But you are safe for the present."

"Slumbers?" The chief *magus* stepped forward. Vima could see the roiling emotions in his expression—gratitude for the salvation of the village, despair arising from his utter failure to find that salvation in the teachings of the prophet. "Will it awaken? What can we do to prevent its return?"

The stranger considered the question for a moment, and then gestured toward the cliff where the demon's cave now looked like just another anonymous pockmark in the stone face. "Though you cannot see it, the darkness is there. What will awaken it, I cannot say, but in the same way that you have defeated it today, you can keep it at bay.

"Consecrate this ground. Make this a sacred place; a place where holy men may contemplate the nature of the cosmos." He paused thoughtfully. "But you must never speak of the darkness, or of what happened here today. Make no record of this occurrence. It is in the nature of men to believe that forces such as this can be controlled, and it may be that in keeping alive the memory of this day, the temptation to awaken the darkness will prove too great to resist. You must let what happened here today slip from your memory, as if something glimpsed in a dream."

Despite the wisdom underlying the admonition, Vima knew that the stranger was asking the impossible. None of the villagers would ever forget this day; how could they? Not only had they all participated in the cataclysmic battle with the demon of darkness, they had also borne witness to the failure of their God. And had not word of the demon's siege on their village spread throughout the empire, carried by travelers along the Silk Road?

No, Vima was quite certain that the events of this day would be spoken of for hundreds, even thousands of years to come.

But Vima was wrong.

In the years that followed, the influence of the *magi* and the teachings of Zoroaster declined as more and more people began to learn the ways of the Enlightened One—the Buddha—and as belief in *Ahura Mazda* waned, so also did the recollection of stories—superstitious fables—about demons and otherworldly entities.

Within two generations, the cliff where a warrior named Vima had once faced an entity of indescribable darkness had become a place where monks carved out caves in which to meditate on the nature of the universe. Three hundred years later, long after the Kushan Empire fell to the Sassanids, and shortly before the subsequent conquest by the Hephthalite Confederation, devotees of the Buddha hewed from the cliff face two extraordinary likenesses of their legendary spiritual leader, thereby unknowingly carrying out the long forgotten stranger's admonition to consecrate the ground where the demon still slept.

It would be nearly fifteen hundred years before darkness of a very different sort would descend upon the land.

SEQUENCE/CONSEQUENCE

1.

Paris, France, 1835 UTC/Local

Bill Downey studied his reflection in the ornate gilt-framed mirror and liked what he saw.

"My goodness," he said, managing what to his ear sounded like a spot-on impression of Cary Grant, "Aren't you just a handsome devil."

He experimented with a few different smiles as he adjusted his bow tie, smoothed the wrinkles from his rented dinner jacket, and then spritzed a few mores ounces of Axe body spray around his neck and throat.

"Oh, yeah," he said to his reflection, now sounding nothing at all like Cary Grant. "Watch out, Paris. I'm getting lucky tonight."

His streak of good luck had actually begun more than two months earlier when, completely out of the blue, he had received an invitation to attend the Global Energy Future meeting in Paris. A lifelong resident of the American Midwest, Downey had never even considered taking a European vacation; his idea of a getaway involved palm trees, fruity cocktails adorned with umbrellas, and lots of women wearing bikinis. But this was an invitation he simply couldn't refuse.

As operations manager of Omaha Public Utility District station 4—a coal-fired 1,200-megawatt producing power plant on the banks of the Missouri River—attending regional conferences was part of the job. The city usually picked up the tab for travel and lodging, and supplied him a stingy per diem, but that hardly made up for the long hours spent poring over charts and statistics in an endless succession of Powerpoint presentations. That the GEF conference was a much higher profile event—not just regional or even national, but global in scale—taking place in the legendary City of Lights, barely made an impression on him...until he read the invitation letter more carefully. Oh, there would be speeches and presentations, but the conference organizer was handling the logistical side, to include business-class air travel and a week's stay at the legendary Hotel Ritz, with complimentary concierge service. The sponsors of the event seemed to have very deep pockets and no compunction regarding how their money was spent. The program for the conference was built around three six-hour days, leaving ample time for site-seeing and nightlife, culminating in what promised to be a spectacular casino event aboard a private riverboat on the Seine. As he reviewed the letter, Downey's first thought had been: *This is too good to be true.* But after another reading, that had changed to: *This is too good to pass up.*

The conference itself had been unremarkable, focusing on vague strategies for dealing with the increasing need for more energy production in developing countries, the importance of retrofitting existing power grids and developing a comprehensive energy policy that included alternative and renewable sources—what Downey thought of as hippy-dippy bullshit. But the short presentations, which he wasn't even obligated to attend, had passed quickly, while the nights had been amazing. The concierge had directed him to the best nightclubs in the city and although he hadn't managed to close the deal with any

Parisian ladies, he'd had a lot of fun trying. All his life, he had heard that the French, and Parisians in particular, were rude, stuck-up and hated Americans, but that had not been his experience. Of course, that might have had something to do with the Platinum AmEx card the conference organizer had given each attendee.

Downey was still primping when an insistent knock disrupted his musings. He shot a glance at his watch. *Six-forty*, he thought. He had arranged to have a car waiting at quarter to seven, but there was no reason not to get a head start on the night's activities. *Odd that they came to the room, but whatever.*

He ambled through the luxurious suite and threw open the door. "You're early…"

His voice trailed off as he found himself once more facing his reflection. No, that wasn't right. A mirror would show a perfect image of him, as he was now, one hand on the doorknob, a quizzical expression on his face. This was something else; him in every detail, standing motionless with a determined, but faintly amused expression. "What the—?"

With an almost unnatural swiftness, the double stepped forward into the suite. With one hand, he swept the door closed behind him. The other hand reached out for Downey, who caught just a glimpse of the oblong black object in the newcomer's hand as it was pressed against his abdomen. A loud crackling sound filled his ears and every muscle in his body contracted instantly. He went rigid and a burning pain spread through his extremities. A moment later, Downey dropped where he stood, his legs folding awkwardly beneath him. He was still conscious, but that mattered little; he felt as if he had been unplugged from his body.

He saw the face that was an almost perfect duplicate of his own hovering above him, but even as he struggled to regain control of his flaccid limbs he felt a sting in the side of his neck and his world quickly dissolved into darkness.

2.

King quickly withdrew the hypodermic needle from Bill Downey's neck and after slipping the safety cap over the glinting metal tip, deposited it in the pocket of his dinner jacket. Then he drew back a few steps and breathed in through his nose, fighting an impulse to sneeze. The fragrance wafting up from the motionless form had triggered some kind of allergic reaction; it smelled like the man had practically bathed in some kind of cologne or body spray. A good sneeze would have been very satisfying, ridding his nostrils of the offending vapors, but the professional make-up artist who had, eight hours previously, transformed King's rugged features into an almost perfect likeness of the power plant manager had cautioned him to avoid any activities that might dislodge the appliqué of latex and cosmetics.

"Sorry you won't be making the party," he told the unconscious man when the irritation in his nasal membranes subsided. "But look on the bright side. I spared you the disappointment of rejection. Here's a tip for next time: subtlety."

King suppressed a chuckle. Laughter was another proscribed action, as was eating, and as he knelt over Downey again, dragging the body over to the neatly made bed, a deep rumble in his gut reminded him of just how hungry he was.

He vividly remembered the last real meal he had eaten, that wasn't a power bar or quickly devoured snack food. Two days earlier, he'd been enjoying a well deserved and much needed day off, relaxing with Sara and Fiona—his family—at a cabin in New Hampshire's Pinckney Bible Conference Grounds, which had been turned back over to the owners and re-opened to the public. Manifold Alpha, the secret base hidden beneath the mountain behind the campground, had been converted to better suit *Endgame*, the new black ops organization of which Chess Team was the core. Endgame had also purchased a number of the cabins, which could be used by personnel for recreation. It had been a strangely perfect day, strange because for the first time in a long time, he hadn't felt like 'King,' hadn't felt like the field leader of an ultra-secret special operations team, but instead had savored the chance to just be Jack Sigler.

Except that wasn't quite right. His Chess Team callsign wasn't an alter ego, a secret identity that he put on and took off like some kind of comic book superhero's costume. He hadn't sublimated the 'real' Jack Sigler to become King. If anything, becoming a spec ops soldier, leading the lethal shooters of Chess Team into dangerous and highly classified missions against the worst kinds of terrorists, literally saving the world from threats that most people would find incomprehensible, was the very essence of who Jack Sigler was.

Or rather, who he had been. Lately, he had begun seeing things from a very different perspective.

Two days ago, hunched over the barbecue grill turning burgers and brats, with his girlfriend Sara lounging nearby sipping a Sam Adams and his foster daughter Fiona exploring the adjacent woods…that was when, for what seemed like the first time in his life, he'd gotten a taste of what it would be like to live as a normal person. And to his complete surprise, he found that he kind of liked it.

He didn't harbor any resentment for the sacrifices he had made in the name of duty, no sorrow for the life he might have had. It wasn't like that at all. He was proud of his service, proud of what Chess Team had accomplished. The world would never know how close or how often it had come to the brink of total destruction. If not for Chess Team, there would be no family vacations, no scenes of domestic tranquility, for anyone at all, and that was not something he took lightly.

From the moment he had enlisted in the Army, galvanized into action by the death of his sister Julie, who had herself answered a similar call by becoming an Air Force fighter pilot, he had never looked back on what might have been. There had been no need. His brothers-in-arms, and particularly his fellow Chess Team operators, were all the family he needed. He had never imagined finding happiness and contentment in a long-term romantic relationship, much less having children of his own. To his surprise, happiness and contentment had found him.

Sara Fogg, an infectious disease investigator for the Center for Disease Control and Prevention, had been his girlfriend for more than two years now. Her job kept her just as busy as Chess Team did him, and from the beginning, they both understood that theirs would be a relationship built on rare treasured moments together. Nevertheless, those moments seemed too few and far between. There was a reason, after all, that relationships were an endangered species in the world of military special operations.

And then there was Fiona.

The teenaged girl had come into his life as a refugee, the lone survivor of a diabolical act of terrorism, hunted by a relentless villain with almost godlike abilities, desperately in need of a protector, but had instead become something much more.

A woman he would be proud to have as a wife and a daughter he cherished... King had accidentally become a family man, and he deeply believed that family deserved more than just stolen moments between missions. Loving someone was a lot more than just protecting that person from harm.

As he had dropped one sizzling bratwurst after another into a line of split stadium rolls, assembling them in an orderly row on a serving platter, he'd considered just what possibilities for happiness the future might hold, and what path to take to get there.

An insistent vibration in his pocket had thrown a monkey wrench into his musings. His phone: Deep Blue on the other end.

"Can't this wait?" King had growled, eschewing the normal pleasantries.

"I'll let you be the judge of that," the reply had come. "We've got him, King. We found Brainstorm."

That had been the end of the picnic.

3.

New Hampshire—Two days earlier

The hamburger King had wolfed down during the short drive from the bungalow to the entrance to Endgame HQ, now sat in his gut like a brick as he waited for the elevator doors to open.

Brainstorm!

Twice now, King had tangled with operatives of what he had dubbed the Brainstorm network, and twice he had narrowly averted unimaginable catastrophe, yet in spite of Brainstorm's audacity, King knew next to nothing about…it? They? The working hypothesis, a construct of innuendo and supposition, was that Brainstorm was a very sophisticated artificial intelligence—a self-aware computer program—secretly pulling the strings of several multinational corporations and possibly exerting influence in the halls of power, but months of investigation had yielded nothing more than rumors and wild conspiracy theories.

The uncertainty about what shape his own future might take didn't include Brainstorm. This was personal.

The steel doors slid back and King hastened down a utilitarian corridor and boarded an underground tram that whisked him to the *Central* portion of the base, ten miles away, under Mount Tecumseh. When he arrived, he disembarked and made his way down another corridor, then burst into the Chess Team op center where Tom Duncan and Lewis Aleman were waiting.

Tom Duncan had once been the leader of the free world—the President of the United States—but King didn't feel like he knew President Duncan. To him, the athletically built, mostly bald Duncan would always be Deep Blue, the creator, brains and guiding hand of Chess Team.

"Well?" King said, even before the door closed behind him. "Let's have it."

Deep Blue nodded, his eyes alight with barely contained enthusiasm. "I'll let Ale fill you in, since he's the one who did all the work."

The lanky Lewis Aleman beckoned King to join him at a workstation. Aleman, a former spec ops shooter and Chess Team's resident tech expert didn't have a callsign, but his unofficial nickname was R2D2, because like the stubby robot from the Star Wars movies, when it came to computer systems, there wasn't much he couldn't accomplish once he plugged in.

"As you know, I've spent the last couple weeks following the money trail from Sokoloff to Brainstorm."

King nodded absently, his thoughts flashing back to the final confrontation with the Russian hitman in the Superstition Mountains of Arizona. Following the brutal struggle, King had found their best lead to unraveling the mystery of Brainstorm—a cell phone that contained a complete record of the hired killer's dealings with the elusive mastermind.

Aleman gestured to the computer monitor, which displayed rows of numbers. "I've had to tread carefully so as not to tip our hand, but I was able to trace the transactions from Sokoloff to an account in the Cayman Islands, and from there to several other accounts."

King gave the list a second look and saw the dollar signs in the second column. Each account balance ran to eight figures. "So Brainstorm has more money than God. That's not exactly news."

The tech expert waved a hand dismissively. "These are just ready cash reserves. Tip of the iceberg. I was able to track dozens of transfers going back two years; Brainstorm, operating through various shell companies, has controlling interests in several multinational corporations, and those assets run well nigh into the trillions. But that's not the point.

"We've been working under the assumption that Brainstorm is an artificial intelligence. I thought that by following the history of the transactions, I'd be able to find a physical location…a bank of computer servers running the AI software."

"But?"

Aleman shook his head, grinning. "It just wasn't there. The transactions didn't originate from any one location. At first, I thought it was just Brainstorm covering its tracks very well, but then something extraordinary happened. Last week, Brainstorm started transferring money out of those accounts—emptied them—and that left a huge footprint."

The undigested burger churned in King's gut. "If Brainstorm is moving that much money around, then it must be planning something big."

"Maybe, but you're missing the point. The money went to a non-profit foundation—Forward Looking Energy Solutions—which it just so happens was the outfit behind Bluelight."

King felt another lurch in his stomach at the mention. The memory of what had happened at the Bluelight Technologies experimental power station was, like the scars on his body, still all too fresh. Bluelight had been attempting to harvest energy from naturally occurring antimatter in the upper atmosphere, a process that had inadvertently summoned a horde of monstrous creatures from an unexplored cave system beneath the Superstition Mountains. King had been investigating the phenomenon when Sokoloff had made his move, and in so doing, had triggered a runaway antimatter reaction that had very nearly set the Earth's atmosphere on fire.

Aleman clicked the mouse controller and brought up the website for something called the "Global Energy Future Meeting."

"FLES—" he pronounced it *fleas*—"is currently hosting a conference for power plant managers from all over the world, ostensibly to discuss ways to upgrade the global power grid, so I was able to learn a lot about them, and in particular, I identified their chief executive officer. It's someone you've met, King. Graham Brown."

An image of Brown flashed up in King's mind's eye; an older, compact figure, reserved and outwardly unthreatening, but confident and enigmatic, as if aware that he held a secret advantage. With his extraordinary ability to calculate mathematical probabilities in his head, Brown had made a small fortune gambling in Atlantic City, and then turned that into a much larger fortune playing the stock market. He had known about the connection between Brainstorm and Brown almost from the beginning—Brown had been present at the remote facility in Algeria where he had first learned of Brainstorm—and there was every reason to believe that Brown had been responsible for creating the artificial intelligence in the first place.

But even as he stared at Aleman, waiting for the man to explain the importance of this connection, King understood. Brown hadn't created...wasn't working for an artificial intelligence called Brainstorm. "Brown *is* Brainstorm?"

A flicker of disappointment crossed Aleman's countenance as King stole his thunder, but he nodded. "It's like a magician using theatrics and distraction to hide the fact that it's all just sleight of hand."

"And it worked," Deep Blue intoned. "Our strategy for dealing with Brainstorm was based on the assumption that it was a non-human entity. We were over thinking it."

"So what's he really up to?" King gestured at the FLES web page. "This interest in new energy technologies would make a lot of sense if we were dealing with a computer. The easiest way to shut it down would be to pull the plug. But what's Brown's angle? And don't tell me he wants to make more money."

Deep Blue grinned broadly, not looking at all like a former Commander-in-Chief. "I guess that's something we'll have to ask him."

King cocked his head sideways. "What have you got in mind?"

Aleman scrolled down the web page revealing a bullet list of highlights for the conference. The last one fairly leapt off the page.

"Casino night," King said aloud.

"Brown's an inveterate gambler. There's no way he'll pass up something like that. And that will be our chance to grab him."

King met Deep Blue's gaze. "So what's the plan?"

4.

Paris, France—1841 UTC/Local

King stared down at the motionless form of Bill Downey—the man into whom he had been transformed by theatrical cosmetics and a high tech auto-tune vocalizing device—and breathed a silent curse. *I hate this* Mission: Impossible *shit.*

The plan Deep Blue had outlined some thirty-six hours earlier, was to gain entry to Brown's casino party by impersonating one of the guests.

"Why not just have Knight reach out and touch him from…say the Eiffel Tower?" Shin Dae-jung, otherwise known as Knight, was Chess Team's designated sniper and the man was exceptionally lethal from a long distance. "I bet he could get a clear shot."

"Normally, I'd be happy to give the go-ahead," Deep Blue had answered without a trace of humor. "It's a kinder fate than Brown deserves. But as you just pointed out, Brainstorm is mobilizing for something big, and we have no idea what it is. Whatever he's up to, the wheels could already be turning. Bringing Brown in alive might be the only chance we've got to put the brakes on."

"We can't exactly arrest him. He's untouchable. He's got his hooks in too many powerful people."

"In a strict legal sense, that might be true, but there are other options available to us." Deep Blue had seemed content to leave it at that, and King had no trouble reading between the lines. And Deep Blue was right about the importance of learning Brainstorm's overarching goal. Brainstorm—or rather Graham Brown—did not do anything on a small scale. He had emptied his cash reserves—in poker parlance, he had gone all in. Perhaps even more telling, he had made virtually no effort to cover his tracks. Brown was unquestionably up to something. They didn't have the first clue what, but if the past was any indication, it would probably mean the end of the world. Ergo, they had to take Brown alive.

Conceptually speaking, their plan was simple. King would impersonate one of the guests and get close enough to Brown to jab him with a tetrodotoxin-tipped needle. The poison, a synthetic version of a toxin found in the internal organs of the puffer fish, would create the appearance that Brown had suffered a fatal heart attack, though in reality he would be in a deep coma, his vital signs slowed to be almost undetectable. Brown's seemingly lifeless body would be taken to a Paris hospital, where some of CIA director Domenick Boucher's most trusted field agents would be waiting. Then, borrowing a page from the Twilight Zone, they would spirit Brown away to a private hospital, and using a combination of play-acting and powerful narcotics, deceive the gambler into giving up all his secrets. After that...well, that was a decision for someone else to make.

Aleman had obtained a list of conference attendees and found one that was a fairly close physical match to King: Bill Downey from Nebraska. A little *Mission: Impossible* shit"—a three-hour session spent with a make-up specialist on loan from the CIA and a little high-tech audio magic from

Aleman—completed the illusion. Shortly thereafter, King boarded a commercial airliner, bound for the City of Lights. The flight had been interminably long. He couldn't eat anything and he didn't dare nod off since either activity might ruin the elaborate facial disguise. His only distraction had been a paperback thriller novel called *The Eden Prophecy*, which he'd picked up at the airport gift shop. He had enjoyed it immensely and made a mental note to check out the author's other novels when the mission was finished.

Speaking of which... He fished out his phone and spoke: "Call Deep Blue."

The voice of the former President sounded in his ear almost immediately. "What's your status?"

"Phase one is complete." The sound of his electronically modified voice—Downey's voice—was mildly disorienting, but he pressed on. "I've made the switch."

As if to punctuate his words, the telephone on the desk trilled with an incoming call.

"I'll call again when it's done." He didn't wait for a reply, but thumbed the 'off' button and snatched up the room phone. "Yes?"

"Monsieur," came a smooth voice. "It is Maurice. Your car has arrived."

"Thank you. I'll be right down."

Showtime.

5.

Fiona Lane gazed out across the treetops at the city skyline. The unfamiliar buildings—and of course the all too familiar outline of the world famous Eiffel Tower—were starting to sparkle with artificial light as the sky darkened from twilight to dusk.

Paris, she thought. *Who would have ever believed I'd be here?*

It was a long way from the obscure reservation town where she'd grown up, a long way from hanging out in front of Noel's Market and drinking milkshakes at the Little Chief diner.

The musing brought a pang of grief. The market and the diner, and everything else—everyone else—in Siletz was gone.

She looked down quickly, blinking back the tears that had welled up, hoping that Sara hadn't seen. The myth of the inscrutable Indian was just that, a myth, but she didn't like showing weakness in front of other people...and especially not in front of King's girlfriend.

King had an assignment to complete in Paris, all very hush-hush like everything he did for Chess Team, but King's boss, the man Fiona still thought of as President Duncan, had decided to surprise King by arranging for Fiona and Sara to join him in the legendary City of Lights for a well-deserved vacation once everything was wrapped up. Fiona had been overjoyed at the prospect and all through the long flight, had felt a thrill of anticipation. But now that was gone, replaced by an overwhelming sadness.

Born and raised in tiny Siletz, Oregon, the idea of visiting Paris seemed like a dream come true. But as they had left the airport and she had gotten her first look at the European city, like a picture book come to life, she had begun to contemplate the unique trajectory of her life that had made this particular dream a reality. Noel's Market and the Little Chief diner...that's where she ought to have been, and but for the tragic events of a few years ago, that's where she still would be. Instead, she had survived the bizarre attack—she alone, while more than three thousand people, including her grandmother, had perished—and been swept up into a new world...a new life. King was her family now, her legal guardian and in every way that mattered, her father. She loved him deeply, but the cost of her new happiness was almost too much to bear.

Three thousand people died... Grandma died... and I get to visit Paris.

She rubbed her eyes, banishing the tears. "I thought there was supposed to be a carousel."

She had to fight to get the words past the lump of emotion in her throat, but if Sara noticed, she gave no indication. Instead, King's girlfriend consulted a tourist pamphlet. "Place du Carrousel," she said after a moment, "gets its name from a type of military review that took place here back in the seventeenth century. Troops on horses, paraded in front of King Louis XIV."

"So, no carousel?"

Sara shook her head, her short spiky hair barely moving with the gesture. "Sorry, kiddo. Just a big park. Want to grab a taxi and head over to the Eiffel Tower?"

That was the last thing Fiona wanted to do. Place du Carrousel, a large circular area between the Louvre Museum and the expansive park known as Jardin des Tuileries, had been in easy walking distance from their hotel and had seemed like the perfect place to stretch their legs after the exhausting flight. A proper visit to the Louvre would require at least a full day, maybe more, but there was plenty to see in the park—monuments and performers. Right now though, Fiona just wanted to crawl into bed and hide from Paris. She turned away from the skyline and let her eyes drift along the current of people moving through the park, some of them on their way to the magnificent Louvre Museum, most of them obviously tourists, just like her.

I'll bet their vacation didn't cost three thousand lives, Fiona thought bitterly.

"No," she said finally. "We should save that for when dad..."

Fiona's voice trailed off as her gaze settled on a tall figure moving purposely through the courtyard. Her eyebrows came together in a crease as she watched the man stride past, not twenty-five yards from where they stood. He bypassed the glittering glass pyramid that decorated the expansive courtyard in front of the main entrance, and continued up the Place du Carrousel toward the busy intersection with the Rue de Rivoli. "What's he doing here?"

Sara looked up from her pamphlet. "What? What's who doing here?"

Curiosity overshadowing her grief, Fiona grabbed Sara's hand. "Come on. Let's follow him."

6.

Julia Preston watched museum visitors come and go from La Chappelle gallery. Like window shoppers perusing the wares in a high-end retail store, they did not linger, and she found their apparent lack of interest discouraging. It was, she supposed, to be expected. People were so utterly predictable. Tourists—and that's what most of them were—did not explore places like the Musée du Louvre with an open mind, eager to make new discoveries, but instead brought their expectations with them, checking items off a list.

See the Mona Lisa. Check. What's next?

She wondered how many of them would, fifteen minutes hence, even remember what they had seen in this room. Few, if any, would grasp its significance, or recognize that they had glimpsed a part of human history that predated Leonardo Da Vinci by nearly a thousand years.

Unlike the pyramids of Egypt or the Acropolis of Athens, the Buddhas of Bamiyan were monuments that relatively few of the planet's inhabitants had been privileged to gaze upon. In the early sixth century, the Hazara occupants of the Bamiyan Valley had carved two monumental statues from the native sandstone, modeling details upon the rock foundation using a traditional composite of mud and straw, covered with stucco. The statues had been noteworthy for being the tallest images of Buddha in a standing pose—the larger of the two measured one hundred and eighty feet—but because of their remote location, eight thousand feet above sea level in Afghanistan, they had not achieved the same level of notoriety as other monumental constructs. Time and weather had worn at the statues, scouring away much of the original detail, but it had been a deliberate act of vandalism that ultimately brought down the Bamiyan Buddhas. In March of 2001, just a few short months before the events of 9/11 plunged the turmoil-prone region back into a state of war, the oppressive Taliban regime, reversed an earlier position that the Buddhas were of historical value and deserving of protection. They had declared the statues to be idols, forbidden by Islam—even though there was not a single Buddhist in the country who might have venerated them—and ordered their destruction.

Following the subsequent overthrow of the Taliban, an effort had been made to restore the Buddhas, but progress had been hampered by the ongoing war, funding problems and international politics. A further complication had arisen in late 2011, when the United States had, in protest of UNESCO's decision to recognize Palestine, withdrawn financial support from the United Nations' cultural agency, which had designated the Bamiyan Valley a World Heritage Site. The traveling museum exhibition, represented a last ditch effort to raise awareness of the flagging restoration effort.

On a technical level, the exhibition was spectacular. It featured state of the art full-sized holographic reproductions of the Buddhas as they would have appeared at the time of their completion. A museum visitor could stand at the foot of the statues and gaze up at the eighteen story high likeness of the

Buddha, never realizing that it was an illusion created by lasers and mirrors. Of even greater significance, at least to Julia's way of thinking, were the countless fragments of the actual statues that had been painstakingly collected from the floor of the Bamiyan Valley, and which now rested in dozens of glass display cases. Most of these pieces were nothing more than chunks of sandstone, scarred and scorched by the barrage of artillery rounds and dynamite charges that had reduced the Buddhas to rubble, but on a few it was still possible to see where ancient craftsmen of the Gandhara Empire had carved the folds of the Buddha's robes.

Yet, for all the technological sophistication and cultural relevance, the exhibition was plagued by the same general apathy that had stymied the restoration effort. Julia had watched museum visitors come and go for several days now; their indifference was almost palpable. But every once in a while, someone would stop and she could see the glimmer of appreciation in their eyes as they read the placards, gazed in awe at the dioramas, and then, almost reverently, placed their hands on the glass display case containing the fragments, as if wishing they could actually touch this part of history.

Her gaze alighted on one figure, a man, who seemed to be taking more than just a passing interest in the exhibit. As she watched, he moved from one display to the next, carefully perusing the descriptive passages before studying the contents. Edging closer, Julia noticed first that the man's silvery-blue eyes were turned to the paragraphs written in English. Then she noticed the handsome face around those eyes.

The eyes shifted ever so slightly, catching her reflection in the glass display case, and then the dark haired man straightened and turned toward her.

Mildly embarrassed at having been caught staring, she hastily tried to deflect his attention. "Tragic, isn't it?"

The corners of the man's mouth tugged up a little into a rueful smile. "That's one word for it," he replied, seeming to agree.

She nodded. "That these marvelous statues could endure the ravages of time for so long, only to be destroyed in a cowardly display of ignorance."

"Cowardly," the man echoed, thoughtfully. "Perhaps. But I don't think ignorance was a factor. The men who destroyed the Buddhas understood all too well the importance of symbols. This was no mere act of vandalism."

"That's a very astute observation." Julia stuck out a hand. "I'm Julia Preston, curator-at-large for the Global Heritage Commission."

The man accepted the proffered hand, holding it gently rather than squeezing it. "Curator-at-large? That sounds very important."

Julia resisted an impulse to giggle. Her title certainly sounded more important than it actually was. In reality, she was more of a glorified handyman, assigned to manage the logistical side of the traveling exhibition. That meant liaising with museum staff—the Louvre was just the first of a dozen museums on the two-year long tour—and making sure that all the moving pieces moved together correctly. It was a far cry from the research and field work that she had dreamed of doing as a graduate student, but it would look very good on her CV.

"You're American?" the man continued.

She nodded.

"Thank goodness. I can get by in French, but anything more complicated than ordering a coffee gives me a headache."

His smile gave her a little thrill. An attractive woman, she had grown weary of fending off the almost predatory advances of Louvre staffers who seemed intent on reinforcing the stereotype of the amorous Frenchman, but somehow she didn't quite feel so ambivalent about a flirtatious exchange with a fellow American—a very attractive and evidently intelligent one at that.

"Your accent," she said, trying to break a little more ice. "There's a bit of Russian there, if I'm not mistaken?"

For just a second, the man's beautiful eyes seemed to darken, but the smile did not falter. "Very perceptive. You're the first person to catch that. As a matter of fact, you're right. I was born in Saint Petersburg, but my parents emigrated to the United States when I was very young. I must have picked it up from them."

"Oh, it's barely noticeable. I'm good at catching accents." Worried that she was only exacerbating the evident *faux pas*, Julia tried to navigate to a different subject. "Are you vacationing in Paris?"

He shook his head. "I'm here for work. But I couldn't pass up a chance to see the Buddhas. My father saw them when he was in the army—the Soviet Army. Three years he served in Afghanistan. He told me all about them and was deeply troubled by their destruction."

She noted that his speech seemed more halting, his accent more pronounced, as if both the unexpected revelation of his origin and the subsequent reminiscence had left him a little shaken. "That's remarkable. I would have loved to have seen them before…" She waved a hand toward the fragments. "Your father must have a unique appreciation for history."

"Yes, and he raised me to have the same appreciation. How does the old saying go? 'Those who don't know history are destined to repeat it.'"

"Edmund Burke." She nodded. "That's sort of the unofficial slogan for historians, and a lesson that we still can't seem to get right. We seem to keep making the same mistakes over and over again."

"As my father is fond of pointing out." The man's eyes turned to the display. "Afghanistan, for example. It has been called 'the place where empires go to die.' Invaders may conquer her armies, but the effort of trying to possess the country is too costly. It destroyed the Soviet Union, but now, only a few decades later, we Americans think our adventure there will end differently."

Julia registered the emphasis he placed on "we Americans," and wondered again if she had somehow inadvertently offended him with her observation about his origins. She wished desperately that she could rewind the encounter and start over, especially since he seemed to share her passion for history. Before she could formulate a response, she glimpsed the familiar figure of Mr. Carutius entering the gallery. She offered a rueful smile. "I'm terribly sorry, but my boss just walked in and I should get to work. But the museum closes just before ten, and I'm not doing anything after…"

She let her voice trail off hopefully. Technically, Carutius wasn't really her boss—she worked for the Global Heritage Commission, an agency adjunct to UNESCO—but inasmuch as he was the chief representative for the private organization that was bankrolling the exhibition, she was pretty much at his beck and call. Carutius was an odd fellow and very hands-on when it came to the nuts and bolts of managing the exhibit. He and his organization had conceived of the idea of taking the fragments of the Buddhas on tour. They had, through generous contributions to Afghanistan's cultural ministry—an agency that existed as little more than a bureaucratic appointment and a way for the corrupt and barely functional government of the beleaguered nation to apportion money received from international aid payments—arranged permission for the shattered remains of the statues to be taken out of the country.

The man matched her smile. "Unfortunately, I have a late business meeting and will be unavailable tonight."

Her mind grappled with his reply. *Unfortunately?* What did that mean? Was he trying to let her down gently, or was he interested in…? "A pity. Another time perhaps. I would really love—" She almost faltered. *Love? Coming on strong, aren't you Julia*—"to sit down and...you know, talk about history a little more."

"I would like that. And I know where to find you."

"I just realized, I never asked your name."

The smile did not waver. "Trevor."

She raised a curious eyebrow, but before she could inquire, he continued: "Not the name my parents gave me when I was born, of course. They changed it when we came to the United States."

Julia nodded in understanding and decided not to press further. "A pleasure to meet you, Trevor. I hope to see you again." She winced inwardly. *God, I sound so desperate.*

But Trevor's smile seemed sincere and when he shook her hand again, it was with the same gentle firmness as at their first meeting, which she took as a good sign. She sighed as he strode from the gallery, then composed herself and went over to where Carutius was rummaging in the large equipment case he had brought in.

Though dressed in an immaculate and expensive Brooks Brothers suit, the tall rugged Carutius, with his curly mop of hair and bushy beard, looked more like an escapee from a biker gang than either a researcher or a financier—Julia wasn't exactly sure which he really was. He glanced up as she approached. "Dr. Preston. I'm glad you're still here. I need to perform some radiometric dating tests on the fragments. We'll need to close the exhibit early tonight."

The man delivered the words with casual indifference, as if he had asked for nothing more complicated than the time of day. Two thoughts immediately raced through Julia's head.

First, why on earth did Carutius want to close the exhibit on a Friday evening, one of the museum's busiest times? How was she supposed to explain to the staff that the much-publicized headlining exhibition, which admittedly had not drawn as much attention as might be hoped, would have to be shut down with no advance notice? If it were anyone but Carutius making the demand, she would have laughed at the very idea.

The second thought was regret that Trevor—or whatever his real name was—had a previous appointment, because now it seemed her evening was free.

"I see," she answered slowly, not seeing at all.

"I've already spoken to the museum director and made all the necessary arrangements," he continued.

Julia felt some relief at that news, and her curiosity gradually got the better of her disappointment. "Do you need any help? What exactly are you hoping to establish with radiometric dating?"

"That won't be necessary. Take the night off."

"The fragments are under the protection of the GHC and we're responsible for their safety. Any requests for testing should go through my office."

"My tests shouldn't pose any risk to the fragments. Quite the opposite, actually." He folded his arms across his chest and although he was smiling, there was no humor in his eyes.

Despite the implicit finality, Julia couldn't just let it go. "I really would like to know what you're testing for."

"It is a personal project and lies at the very heart of my interest in preserving the Buddhas. Something I've been working on for years. I'm sorry, but that's all I can tell you." He loosed one arm and gestured to the exit. "Good night, Dr. Preston."

7.

Timur Suvorov replayed his conversation with Dr. Julia Preston—the curator knew him only as "Trevor"—in his head as he stalked through the corridors of the Louvre, and wondered where he had slipped up. His instructors at the cultural immersion training facility had praised him for his pitch perfect English and his command of American dialect, but she had picked up on his true heritage after hearing him say only a few words.

Suvorov had never actually been to the United States. The closest he had come to that experience was a six-month long stay in a town called Springfield, a perfect middle-American suburb that happened to be located, not in the American heartland but in a remote location on the coast of the Caspian Sea.

Springfield had been built during the Cold War by the KGB for the sole purpose of training long-term deep cover operatives—sleepers, in the common parlance—who would be able to perfectly blend into American society. Every aspect of life in Springfield had been simulated Americana, at least insofar as the Soviet social scientists understood it. The only language spoken in the mock-city was English. The radios played a wide selection of American music and American television programs were broadcast. Residents could get Big Macs at the local McDonald's and bought their cigarettes and Coca-Colas at the 7-Eleven. Thousands of KGB sleepers had literally been raised from infancy in Springfield, and many graduates of the program had subsequently been deployed to conduct active espionage or, more often than not, await a critical assignment that would never come. In the post-Cold War era, Russia's foreign intelligence service, the SVR, continued to conduct operations abroad. But these days there were more expedient methods of getting agents into place, particularly with the advent of globalization and a growing population of Russian expatriates in America and other countries. Nevertheless, Springfield continued to be useful as a training tool for SVR operatives and GRU Spetsnaz soldiers preparing for undercover work.

Evidently there were still some gaps in the training though, as Julia's observation had borne out.

In retrospect, it had probably been a bad idea to visit the museum. To establish their cover stories and blow off a little steam before the final phase of the assignment, Suvorov had directed the members of his team to do a little site seeing. Despite the stereotypical Russian proclivity for alcohol consumption, drinking was strictly forbidden before an operation, as was sexual congress, but there were plenty of other distraction in the City of Lights, and for Suvorov, a chance to see the Bamiyan Buddhas, even if they were now only pieces of rubble, had seemed the obvious choice.

The lie he had told to cover his dismay at Julia's revelation was close enough to the truth to satisfy the woman's curiosity. He had indeed been born in Saint Petersburg—in his earliest memories, it was still called Leningrad—and his father really had seen the Buddhas during his military service. Her discovery nonetheless posed a risk for potential exposure moving forward. When she learned of the operation in the news, would she put two and two together, and perhaps report her suspicious encounter with a man claiming to be a Russian émigré? Probably not, but it was best not to leave such a thing to chance. Julia was a loose end that would have to be tied up, one way or another, and he found that thought discouraging.

Actually, there was a lot about this mission that troubled him.

No, that wasn't quite right. Not just this mission; he'd been experiencing misgivings about everything in his life. The sense of pride he'd once felt in his military service, in excelling in his training and commanding a team of Russia's very best special operations soldiers, in literally being a part of shaping the future of the *Rodina*…those ideological concepts just didn't square with reality. That was another lesson of history. Brave men—his team, and even his father before him—were always the ones who made the sacrifices, while the politicians who sent them to their appointments with destiny were always chasing some selfish agenda. This mission was no different. They would succeed of course, but in the end, would it make any difference?

He reached the main exit, threading past the idling masses of tourists, and once outside took out his phone and called Kharitonov. When his subordinate answered, he spoke only two words: "It's time."

8.

King took a deep breath as he stepped off the gangplank and onto the reception deck of the riverboat. The vessel was anchored in the Seine about four hundred yards southwest of Île Saint-Louis. King could just make out the French Gothic silhouette of the Notre Dame Cathedral on the nearby Île de la Cité, against the background of the dazzling electric Parisian skyline.

A score of men in formal attire milled about sipping cocktails and smoking cigars, and vying for the attention of a scattering of attractive women in expensive evening gowns. King guessed the latter group to be professional escorts; even without Aleman's report on the guest list indicating that not a single woman had been invited to the FLES conference, King observed that they were too attractive, too confident in their sexuality and perhaps most tellingly, too young, to be anything else.

Although he had been wearing Bill Downey's face for several hours now, there had been no opportunity to test its effectiveness in fooling people who actually knew the man.

There was no way to know if Downey had befriended fellow conference attendees, or if those acquaintances would immediately notice the less obvious indicators—mannerisms, his walk, his sense of humor—that would give him away. He had already resolved to avoid contact with other guests as much as possible, but in the confines of the floating casino, that was easier said than done.

Pushing down his anxiety, he skirted the edges of the gathering. His route took him past the bar, where he reluctantly turned down the offer of a drink—a shot of Booker's sounded pretty tempting—and bypassed a table loaded with a smattering of hors d'oeuvres. His stomach rumbled in protest as he glanced at the dishes of Beluga caviar, the plates of *pâté de foie gras* and an assortment of breads and cheeses, and he decided that, once Brown was in the bag, so to speak, he'd have to take advantage of the spread. Closer to the door, King passed a table where a steward was dispensing cigars, and helped himself to a brace of Partagás, which he slipped into the pocket of his dinner jacket. *Rook will like these*, he thought, *if…no, make that when, he turns up.*

As he finished at the cigar table, King took a moment to study the crowd. Brown was not in evidence—no surprise there. He quickly identified several men who looked every bit as out of place as the women. A few were dispersed throughout the crowd, but most were hanging at the edges, avoiding conversation as their eyes roamed the assemblage. Their muscular physiques, which seemed to strain the cut of their dinner jackets, and rigid bearing marked them as military types, and King figured them for security personnel, probably from the ranks of Alpha Dog—the same mercenary outfit that Brainstorm had employed in Africa. King curtailed his own surveillance to avoid drawing the attention of the hired guns, and moved toward the double doors leading into the riverboat's main saloon.

King paused at the entrance to survey the room. He vaguely

noted the rich appointments—red velvet walls with oak wainscoting, crystal chandeliers and the gleam of brass wall sconces. It all starkly contrasted with the garishness of the electronic slot and video poker machines that lined the edges of the room. The machines seemed to be the primary focus of attention for partygoers, who were no doubt drawn in by the lights and sounds and their own familiarity with the devices. The rest of the space had been divided equally between different table games, predominantly those favored by American gamblers—blackjack, craps, roulette, and Texas Hold 'em poker—with a half-dozen or so gamblers trying their luck at each. At the far end of the room, a musical ensemble played subdued jazz from a low dais. King's quickly picked out the security men, but again there was no sign of Brown.

To kill time, he sidled over to the cashier and produced Downey's Platinum AmEx. The attractive woman shook her head. "No need for that, sir. The house has extended a ten thousand dollar line of credit to all guests."

"Ten thousand?" King replied, conversationally. "I wonder how long it will take me to lose that."

She flashed a flirtatious smile, and then pushed a stack of rectangular chips across the green felt surface. "Maybe this will be your lucky night."

King grinned back, feeling the rubbery make-up on his cheeks crinkling in protest. "You have no idea."

Idly shuffling the stack of chips, he moved to the blackjack tables and took a seat. He wasn't much of a gambler. He didn't even buy lottery tickets. Although soldiering was, by its very nature, the ultimate gamble, he had survived in his chosen profession by minimizing risks. It was no coincidence that his elite squad had chosen "Chess Team" as an operational callsign. Chess was primarily a game of skill and attention to detail, not a test of random luck. And while military operations, like chess games, could not be won without taking some bold risks, a skillful strategist could accurately predict the outcomes and almost always choose the course of action that would win the day. In casino games, the only thing that was certain was that the odds were always stacked in favor of the house.

Still, it wasn't like there was any risk here; win or lose, it wasn't his money to begin with.

He played through several hands, betting conservatively and winning only occasionally. Anyone observing would have thought his slightly hunched posture to be indicative of an intense focus on the game, but in reality, he barely watched the progression of cards flashing across the table or noticed his dwindling stack of chips. His gaze flitted back and forth across the room, watching for Brown to make an appearance, and as the hour wore on, he began to wonder if the operation wouldn't prove to be, in gambling terms, a bust.

Then, promptly at eight o'clock, the music ceased and a voice crackled from the public address system, directing everyone to gather in the casino. Immediately, people began streaming in from the deck, raising the ambient noise level in the room to a low tumult. King played out the hand in progress, standing on nineteen and winning, and then scooped up his chips and made his way through the milling herd to the stage where the musicians were putting away their instruments. A few moments later, the man himself—Graham Brown, aka: Brainstorm—ascended the dais with a wireless microphone in hand, and the room broke into spontaneous applause. King joined in, unenthusiastically patting his hands together as he studied the face of his nemesis.

9.

Fiona had caught a final glimpse of the tall man entering the side entrance of the Louvre, but her attempt to follow was immediately thwarted by a security guard. He haughtily informed her, in halting and heavily accented English, that the ticket window at Passage Richelieu was closed and that entry was only possible at the Pyramid entrance or from the Carrousel du Louvre—an underground shopping mall that connected the museum with several other noteworthy landmarks.

"You let that other guy through," Fiona had protested.

"Mr. Carutius? He has official business. He is not a tourist." *Like you.* The guard had made no effort to hide his irritation at having to explain himself to a lowly American visitor, and a child at that.

"What kind of business?"

"He is the administrator of the special exhibit." The guard then made a shooing gesture and stepped back to his post.

It had taken nearly half an hour for Fiona and Sara to make their way back around to Place du Carrousel and through the line to the ticket window; plenty of time for Sara to demand an explanation. It occurred to Fiona that King might not have told Sara about the man who now seemed to be calling himself "Carutius."

"It's Hercules," she said simply. "You know about him?"

Sara's expression was guarded. "You mean Alexander Diotrophes, the leader of the Herculean Society?"

So he has told her. "That was him I saw, going into the museum."

Sara gave her a pinched expression. Fiona could sense the looming question, *Are you sure?* But instead Sara said, "The Louvre has one of the largest collections of antiquities in the world. It's not so strange that Diotrophes would have business here. It's got to be a coincidence."

"Whenever he's around, there's trouble," Fiona declared.

"That's not exactly a compelling rationale for chasing after him," Sara countered. Nevertheless, King's girlfriend made no move to pull Fiona out of the line. Instead, when her turn came, she forked over fourteen Euros—as a minor, Fiona's ticket was free—and grabbed a brochure containing a rough map of the complex.

"Where's the special exhibit?" Fiona tapped her foot impatiently as Sara unfolded the pamphlet, flipped it around then back again. "Well?"

"Fi, there are half a dozen special exhibits: The Mariette Collection; the Da Vinci sketches; the relics of Saint Caesarius of Arles; the Bamiyan Buddhas...Where do you want to start?"

Fiona let out a low growl. "How should I know?"

Sara blinked at her impassively for a moment, but then seemed to grasp Fiona's frustration. "Look, most of these exhibits are in the Sully Wing. That's the closest section to us right now. We'll work our way through them one by one, okay?"

Fiona nodded gratefully and walked beside Sara as they made their way from the lobby. Her eyes roamed the faces of museum patrons, searching for Hercules—Diotrophes, or Carutius or whatever he was calling himself—but there was no sign of the man. He would be hard to miss, standing a head taller than most men, with his distinctive hair and beard. Yet, as much as she was focused on her search, her eyes were drawn to the elaborate décor of the former royal palace and to the *objets d'art* displayed everywhere, which surprised her.

She'd never been particularly interested in classical art. Her own heritage had ingrained in her an appreciation for a much different style of expression, one that was to her way of thinking more honest, much more in harmony with the natural world and deserving of more honor than these paintings and sculptures with which the rest of the world seemed so enamored. But despite the fact that she had entered the museum for a very different reason, she found her gaze almost magnetically attracted to the displays and her pace began to falter.

She quickened her step, catching up to Sara as the latter reached the entrance to a gallery sporting a banner advertising the relics of Saint Caesarius of Arles. Sara ventured a few steps inside. "Big guy, right?" she said. "I don't see him."

Fiona did not answer. She knew she should be surveying the scattering of visitors, looking for Hercules, but she found herself unable to look away from a marvelous box of gold encrusted with jewels and positioned directly in front of the entrance. Something about the beautiful reliquary absorbed her attention, filled her with an almost transcendent euphoria...

"Fi?"

Fiona shook her head, breaking eye contact with the relic box, and the feeling receded. "No, he's not here."

"Let's try the Da Vinci sketches, next." Sara seemed not to have noticed the girl's fascination with the reliquary. "That's the kind of thing Diotrophes would be interested in, right?"

Fiona nodded dumbly and followed along, but she now kept her gaze on the floor, purposefully resisting the urge to visually take in her surroundings. She was only peripherally aware of the route Sara navigated, and in the back of her mind, it occurred to her that if they became separated, she wouldn't have a clue how to find her way out. A few moments later, Sara stopped and Fiona looked up to see another gallery awaiting their inspection.

The large room was a veritable maze of freestanding display cases, each containing pages of vellum, adorned with delicate script and what looked like pencil sketches. Above the cases were enlarged reproductions of select images, the subjects ranging from detailed human figures to elaborate machines, and not a few bizarre creatures that looked to Fiona like they might contain hidden figures in the illustrated folds of skin and fur—like something from a child's Find It puzzle. Fiona experienced a mixture of relief and disappointment as she gazed at the enormous prints; they did not produce the reaction she had felt in the other gallery.

And then her eyes fell on the original sketches.

She barely heard Sara say: "I don't see him here, do you?"

Fiona worked her mouth, trying to form the question that had bubbled into her head but it was an effort. "Sara, you know your sensory whatever-it-is? How you can 'see' smells and stuff?"

Sara Fogg had been diagnosed with Sensory Processing Disorder; her sensory neural pathways didn't always function the way they should, causing her to experience stimuli in unpredictable ways—to 'smell' colors or feel twinges of pain when seeing certain objects. Fiona had heard Sara and King talk about it from time to time, but she didn't really understand the details.

"Sure." A note of concern haunted Sara's answer.

"Is it contagious?" Fiona pressed.

"Absolutely not. Fi, what's wrong?"

Fiona gazed at the Da Vinci sketches, her eyes flitting back and forth as if trying to take all of them in all at once. The drawn images seemed to burst off the parchment and the

carefully scripted notes glittered like magical runes in a Tol-
kien novel, imparting mystical knowledge that she could not
read, but somehow intimately understood.

"I think I must have it too," she said after a breathless
moment. "Because these pictures are singing to me."

10.

Despite his stylish dinner jacket and immaculately coiffed silver hair, Graham Brown seemed no less banal a personage than he had in his first and only other encounter with King, in the remote Algerian villa where Sara Fogg had briefly been held prisoner.

Brown waited for the applause to die down before lifting the microphone and addressing the crowd. "Is everyone having fun spending my money?" he quipped, triggering a symphony of cackles and guffaws, and another round of clapping.

"Seriously folks," he continued, sounding to King's ear like a cut-rate stand-up comedian, "I don't want to keep you from the festivities, but I just wanted to take this opportunity to thank you all for traveling here, from every corner of the globe, to take part in our little symposium.

"Power. It's the reason we're all here. And I'm not just talking about electrical energy. In times past, human society hungered for literal food, but now our greatest need is for the energy to drive our machines and our electrical devices. We have become entirely dependent on technology, and if the energy supply that makes it function were to be interrupted, it would be a disaster far worse than any famine or drought. Power, real power, belongs to those who can control the energy supply. And you, my friends, have that power."

King listened attentively as Brown seemed on the verge of launching into a megalomaniacal diatribe, and he noticed others in the crowd murmuring uncomfortably.

"Or perhaps to put it more accurately," Brown continued, softening his rhetoric. "You are the faithful stewards of that power. Society has entrusted the care and protection of its future to you, but make no mistake: it is a great responsibility. The power, of which I speak, does not rest with any one of us, nor with any man, nation or corporation. Nevertheless, it is something unscrupulous men might desire, and that is where we are vulnerable.

"I organized the Global Energy Future conference to call attention to this vulnerability. Our stewardship requires that we protect our trust—this great and potentially terrible power— from those who might seek to seize control for some dark purpose. As you are all doubtless aware, much of our power grid relies on early 20th century technology. The transmission of electricity through copper wires, for example, where ninety-nine percent of the energy is lost to resistance. The use of decades old computer systems for managing the grid. These are but two examples of challenges we must address if we are to meet the needs of the future.

"What we have done here this past week is merely to state the nature of the problem, but I'd like to think that we have also explored some possible solutions. Many of the technologies we've showcased are still in the conceptual phase. Others are presently too expensive to meet the demands of economic efficiency. Nevertheless, we must be willing to take some risks.

"It's no coincidence that I have chosen to close the week's activities with this casino event. Gambling is the perfect meta-phor for the challenge we face. Will we play it safe? Stand on seventeen? Or will we take bold risks, losing sometimes, but in the end, winning the jackpot?

"I hope you will consider this metaphor as you return to your homes and your jobs. The safe bet, the status quo, is a slow path to failure. And the stakes are very high, my friends."

Brown lowered the microphone, and on cue, the gathering clapped again, but this time the applause was more subdued, respectful rather than enthusiastic. The host however was not quite finished.

"Now, as a way of repaying you for having to suffer through my little speech, I have a little surprise." Brown looked offstage and nodded to one of the stewards. "As I mentioned, there are some fantastic new technologies that aren't quite ready for widespread distribution, but one of them is now ready for some real world field testing."

As he spoke, a line of stewards trekked onto the stage and hastily deployed a folding table, upon which they deposited two elegant, covered, silver serving trays. When they had finished, Brown stepped behind the table and took a piece of paper from his pocket. "Would the following men please join me on stage?"

King's curious musings about the contents of the serving trays were interrupted when he heard Brown speak the name of the man whose face he now wore. After overcoming his surprise and dismay, he jolted into motion.

As he moved onto the stage, King's thumb brushed the ring on his third finger of his right hand, spinning the band around so that its decorative face was toward his palm. The ring, a Cold War-era spy gadget on loan from the CIA—probably from their museum—concealed the poison-tipped needle that would, if all went according to plan, take Brown permanently out of circulation. A gentle tap on the jeweled head—the pressure of a handshake or a squeezing grasp on the upper biceps, perhaps the result of an attempt to arrest a feigned stumble—would thrust the spring-loaded needle into its target.

He might not get this close to Brown again.

King played the scenario out in his mind as he strode forward. *Too obvious*, he decided. *Too many people watching.* He couldn't afford to attract attention or raise suspicions. The boat was crawling with Alpha Dog security guards. The ring was his only weapon and it had only one dose of tetrodotoxin, just enough to bag the objective.

Be patient. You'll get another chance.

Nevertheless, he could feel his skin burning with rage beneath the disguise as he passed behind Brown. The man had kidnapped Sara. He'd sent a hired killer after King in Arizona. And in his quest for—*what exactly?*—he'd very nearly eradicated all life on the planet, not once but twice.

But then he passed Brown and stood with the others—ten of them altogether—waiting to see what surprises the man had in store.

The host faced them, speaking once more into the microphone. "I've chosen you from the group because each of you manages a large power plant, and as such are in a unique position to benefit from my little gift."

Plant managers, King thought. Was this part of Brainstorm's master plan? *Damn, I should have paid attention to the names.*

With a flourish, Brown removed the domed covers to reveal ten small black rectangular boxes arrayed on swatches of red velvet. King blinked, tearing his gaze away from Brown, and glanced at the offering.

"Cell phones?" remarked one of the other men, with more than a trace of disappointment.

Brown smiled patiently and picked up one of the rectangles. "Appearances can be deceiving. This device may look like an ordinary cellular phone, but trust me when I say that it has as much in common with the iPhone or Droid in your pocket, as those devices do with an old-fashioned rotary dial telephone.

Those devices have been called 'smart phones.' Well, gentleman, this…" He held it up, turning to the rest of the audience, "is a *genius* phone.

"It's actually much more than just a telecommunications device. Don't let its size fool you. Each of these little boxes holds more computing power than the mainframe networks that most of you are probably using at your plants."

There were a few skeptical glances, but Brown continued without missing a beat. "Witness the next evolution of the computer: the quantum processor, courtesy of my new friends at Jovian technologies. Instead of using printed silicon chips, these devices carry out calculations at the atomic level. That's how we're able to get so much computational power into such a small package. But that's only part of it. Quantum processing speeds also make it possible to utilize a remarkable new 'stutter logic' artificial intelligence interface."

King raised an eyebrow at the mention of artificial intelligence, and recalled their original supposition about Brainstorm. Was that Brown's game? Was he trying to create the independent computerized entity that he had, for so long, pretended to be?

"I can't give you all the specifics," Brown went on. "I'm not a 'techie' myself. But this AI application streamlines the user interface. No more logic errors or confusion about trying to figure out the correct sequence of operations. You just tell the computer what you want—it responds to either voice or text commands—and it can figure out what you're really asking. It probably understands better than another human would.

"Gentleman, these devices aren't just for checking your e-mail or downloading YouTube videos. With just one of these, linked to your existing mainframe, you could single-handedly run your power plants, at least insofar as the computerized systems are concerned. In fact, you could do it from anywhere in the world." Brown smiled, then after a thoughtful pause, added: "And of course, they are fully functional phones, too."

"Oh great," said one of the other men with mock sarcasm. "Wouldn't you know it? I just signed a two-year contract with T-Mobile."

Brown swept up the quantum phones and began distributing them to the men. "Not to worry. They are completely compatible with your existing phone carriers. The quantum processor can wirelessly synch with the phone you are now using—just hold it next to your phone, turn it on and tell it what you want to do."

King watched as the other men eagerly followed Brown's advice, and took out their personal phones. For his part, he simply dropped the new acquisition into his pocket where it joined the cigars he had pilfered earlier. Aleman would get a kick out taking the gizmo apart.

With the presentation of the quantum phones complete, the recipients began folding back into the crowd, eager to show off the unique devices. The men closest to Brown managed to buttonhole their host, and were expounding on some of their pet ideas for retrofitting the power grid. King lined up behind them, absently twirling the ring, and waited for his chance. A few interminable minutes later, he heard Brown excuse himself, preparing to move away.

King seized the opportunity, pushed past the other guests and stuck out his hand.

11.

Less than fifty feet away, in a cramped room surrounded by flat screen monitors, Bandar Pradesh watched the live video feed of the ten power plant managers receiving their new quantum phones. He glanced to another monitor that displayed the status of the quantum network.

Brown had omitted mention of the fact that the phones themselves did not actually contain quantum processors, or rather, did not contain complete, independent processing units. In fact, it was a bit misleading to use standard computer jargon to explain the functionality of a quantum computer, but that was something Brown had never really been able to grasp. Like most people, the man was unable to conceive of a world that was not governed by Newtonian cause-and-effect mechanics. Conventional computers relied completely on principles of physical logic—if-then relationships, ones or zeroes—but quantum computers utilized an entirely different set of rules where those relationships had no meaning whatsoever.

Of course, it wasn't necessary for Brown to understand the technology, any more than it was necessary for every automobile owner to understand the function of an internal combustion engine. In fact, Pradesh thought, it was probably better that he didn't seem to want to know. That had made it so much easier for the Indian computer genius to accomplish his real objective.

Pradesh watched as the number of users on the network jumped from two to six...then to eight, then nine, and he waited for the tenth and final user to go active. The network relied on multiple inputs for operation. Moreover, the system was its most effective when those input nodes were linked randomly to existing conventional networks, so it was not enough to simply build several devices and turn them on. To make the quantum computer fulfill its purpose, Pradesh had designed the computer to utilize ten nodes, all connected to the worldwide communications network via their independent users. More would have been better, but given the prohibitive cost of producing the devices and the dictates of Brown's original plan, ten would have to suffice.

The number on the screen did not change.

Pradesh watched it with growing impatience, and then turned his attention to the closed-circuit television screen where he saw the ten men were busily downloading new applications and exploring other features. *No*, Pradesh realized. *Not all of them.*

He isolated the one man in the group who was not holding one of the devices, and consulted the guest list. "Downey," he muttered. "Why aren't you playing with your new toy?"

On an impulse, he zoomed in on the man's face and ran the image through a battery of tests. To his surprise, the facial recognition software—a variation of the same program used by casinos to identify card-counters and other troublemakers— indicated a less than seventy-percent probability that the man in the image was actually Bill Downey.

Frowning, Pradesh rolled back the footage to the moment where Downey walked onto the stage and tried a different program. This software ignored facial characteristics and focused instead on body mechanics, comparing the way the man moved to both the real Bill Downey and to an exhaustive database collected from security feeds in travel hubs around the world. If this man had taken a commercial flight anytime in the last five years, his distinctive gait and mannerisms would be in the database.

He immediately got a hit from a flight originating from New York less than twenty-four hours earlier. Not Downey though—the real Downey had been in Paris all week, and this man wasn't a match anyway. Then another hit came up, and this time it was accompanied by an urgent message, flashing in red letters.

Pradesh stared in disbelief for a moment before following the instructions in that message. He took out his phone and made a call. "There is a complication," he said as soon as the connection went through. "King is here."

"King?" came the reply. "He's still alive? Brown was a fool to think that piece could be so easily taken off the board. But this game between Brown and King has no bearing on our objective."

"You don't understand," Pradesh persisted. "He is in disguise as one of the ten."

There was a long silence. "So?"

"He isn't activating his node. He appears to have no interest in it. He put the device in his pocket."

"That is a complication," admitted the man at the other end of the line. Another thoughtful pause. "But there is a simple solution. I'm sure Brown will be very interested to know that Jack Sigler has crashed his party."

12.

King straightened his fingers so that his hand was completely flat, a necessary precaution to avoid accidentally injecting himself with the poison.

For a fleeting second, he saw success sitting squarely in his crosshairs. Brown took a phone call on his headset, raising an index finger to say he'd just be a minute. With the call completed, he turned back to King, his lips turning up ever so slightly in a smile. King thought he saw the man's shoulders shift...was he about to extend his hand, accept the handshake? A moment later, he understood the reason for the smile. Then he felt powerful hands close around his biceps and forearms. King instinctively struggled against the grip, but now saw a pair of Alpha Dog guards on each side of him.

Brown's smile transformed into something hard and grim. "Don't make a scene, Sigler. I spent a lot of good money on this little soiree, and I'd hate for you to ruin it."

King's heart started pounding in his chest. This wasn't merely a minor reversal; his mission had just gone from textbook to FUBAR. Somehow, Brown had discovered him.

They must have found the real Downey, he thought. But no,

even if that were the case, he'd left no clues pointing back to his real identity. *How then?*

Brown leaned close to one of the hirelings and whispered: "Take him below and put a bullet in his head. Nothing clever, just kill him. We can dispose of the body later."

Before King could even think about offering further resistance, the mercenaries lifted him a few inches off the ground and began walking him off the stage.

In desperation, King shouted: "You're forgetting something, Brainstorm."

His captors' stride remained unfaltering as they stepped down from the dais and angled toward a door at the rear of the saloon.

"You should hear what I've got to say," he shouted over his shoulder, but Brown was already turning away. "You think we don't know what you're really up to? My team is standing by, ready to shut you down."

If Brown heard him there was no reaction.

He chose his next words very carefully, shouting them even as he was hustled through the door. "What's the probability that I'm bluffing?"

His words seemed to echo in the now awkwardly quiet room, but then the door closed behind him and there was no one to hear his protests except for the four dour guards. He considered trying to reason with them, but one look told him that would be fruitless. He knew their ilk well: former military, probably separated under dubious circumstances. In love with guns and killing, but not so good at discipline or observing rules of engagement. Shaved heads, muscle-bound and faces a little puffy from steroid use. He wondered if they would draw straws for the privilege of administering the killing shot.

As soon as the door closed, they set him down, but before he could even think about trying to twist out of their collecting grasp—a plan unlikely to succeed, but better to go down fighting—something hard crashed into the back of his skull. His last thoughts were of Sara and Fiona—sadness over never seeing them again, and relief that they were safe at home—then darkness claimed his mind.

13.

The sound of voices drew King back to consciousness—one voice in particular. The return to consciousness was a pleasant surprise and almost made up for his splitting headache. If he was still alive, then maybe Brown had fallen for his last ditch ploy.

But all he had accomplished was to postpone the inevitable; he needed a plan.

"You are not hearing what I'm saying," came one voice—a man, but high pitched, with a faintly sing-song accent that suggested the speaker might be from India or one of the surrounding countries. "All we need to do is turn it on and sync it to another phone. Any phone will do."

"There is a sixty-two point three percent probability of success if the network is brought to active status in that configuration. The probability increases to eighty-eight point seven if the desired configuration is achieved."

Although this second voice—flat, almost mechanical in its intonations—was not familiar to King, he immediately recognized it from what was said. This was what had brought him out of the darkness. The statements of probability, seemingly generated by a computer… This was the electronically generated voice of Brainstorm.

He remained motionless with his eyes closed, trying to hide the fact that he was now awake. He was seated and the ache in his arms told him that his hands were bound, his arms wrapped around the back of a chair. Something felt different about his face, and when he worked his jaw experimentally, he realized that the disguise had been removed. *Thank goodness for small favors*, he thought. *If I get out of this, I swear, no more* Mission: Impossible *shit.*

"If we don't bring the network on-line, then the probability of success is zero," protested the first voice. "We shouldn't wait."

"Your concern is noted, Mr. Pradesh. However, the timeline does not indicate a necessity for precipitous action."

"I think he's waking up." A third voice intruded into the conversation, this one low and rough, and King surmised that one of the mercenary guards had noticed him stirring. Still feigning disorientation, King raised his head and looked around.

He was in an office, richly appointed in a style similar to the casino, but without any personal touches that might have offered insights into the man who now held him captive. Graham Brown, still looking dapper in his tuxedo, sat behind a solid looking desk a few feet away, his fingertips steepled together as if in deep thought. The desktop was uncluttered, as though the office had never been used, but King noted two conspicuous objects: the quantum computer device he had been given earlier and his own cell phone, his lifeline to Endgame HQ.

Three other men occupied the office. Two were burly figures in formal wear—security personnel—one of them sitting casually on the edge of the desk, the other in a chair to King's left. The third, sitting to King's right, was a small, lean man with black curly hair and dark skin, dressed in chinos and a polo shirt. *That would be Pradesh,* King thought. The name was familiar, but he couldn't quite remember where he had heard it.

King brought his gaze back to Brown. "So much for just killing me," he remarked.

Brown evinced no reaction whatsoever. His eyes did not flicker and he did not speak. A moment later, the flat electronic voice issued from a speakerphone on one corner of the desktop. "A cost-benefit analysis determined that you are of more value alive, Mr. Sigler."

King laughed, sending a fresh wave of pain through his skull. "I certainly think so."

"Point one," the voice continued, as if King's quip had been an inquiry. "Your actions here are offensive in nature. There is only a thirty-four point two percent probability that you would undertake such action without support. You are, in all likelihood, only one member of a team, perhaps similarly disguised and currently moving freely about the interior of this vessel. It is a further likelihood that your death would bring about an immediate reprisal, whereas concern for your health and safety may presently be a factor in preventing an incursion."

There was no little irony in the fact that he was alive only because Brainstorm had overestimated him. The truth was, it had been foolish to go in without back-up. *God damned* Mission: Impossible *shit.* "That's a lot of words to say I'm more valuable as a hostage."

"Point two: You employed a disguise to infiltrate this location. The probability that this action is sanctioned by French law enforcement authorities is twelve point one percent. In other words, Mr. Sigler, you are trespassing. Your death, while imminently justifiable, would lead to undesirable legal entanglements."

King studied Brown as the voice droned on. The man was absolutely unflappable. "Amazing," King interjected. "I can't even see your lips move."

In fact, Brown's implacability was troubling. The entire mission had been conceived with the belief that Brown *was* Brainstorm; that the artificial intelligence was just a clever distraction—a ventriloquist's dummy, as King had just intimated. Yet, Brown was sitting there, almost completely motionless, while Brainstorm carried on independently. How was that possible? Had Aleman and Deep Blue erred in their assessment of the true nature of Brainstorm?

"Point three: You are impersonating William Maxwell Downey, a guest of the Global Energy Future conference. I would like to know what happened to Mr. Downey."

King didn't answer. He recalled the earlier conversation between Brainstorm and Pradesh. *All we need to do is turn it on and synch it to another phone,* Pradesh had said. *Any phone will do.*

The quantum phone had been meant for Downey.

King recalled the rest: *There is a sixty-two point three percent probability of success if the network is brought to active status in that configuration. The probability increases to eighty-eight point seven if the desired configuration is achieved.*

Downey. The quantum phones. What was the connection? He let this point slide, curious to see what else Brainstorm would reveal.

"There are, however, compelling arguments for your immediate termination. Counterpoint one: While your successful interference with the project in Africa appeared to be a statistical outlier, it seemed prudent to arrange your termination. Your subsequent destruction of the Bluelight facility in Arizona, as well as your now apparent survival of Mr. Sokoloff's assassination attempt, have shifted the mean probability assessment regarding the likelihood of future interference. Or to express this in terms that Mr. Brown might use, leaving you alive for any length of time is pushing my luck."

Bluelight, a new energy technology...power plant managers... More pieces clicked together, but the big picture remained maddeningly obscure.

"Counterpoint two: The probability that you will voluntarily elect to reveal factual information about your present operation, the size, location and identity of your allies in this incursion, or Mr. Downey's whereabouts, is effectively zero. Mr. Steeves, my head of security, is of the opinion that he can persuade you to talk by utilizing enhanced interrogation techniques—"

King spat out derisive laughter.

"—but time is a factor and it is probable that, even with such methods, you would seek to deceive or obfuscate."

King expected the list to continue, but the electronically produced voice fell silent, prompting him to speak. "So you've decided to keep me around a little while longer, is that right?"

"The risk-benefit analysis indicates that to be the most efficient course of action. However, as I have indicated, the potential benefit is moderated by temporal considerations."

"So, if I don't tell you what you want to know soon, there's no reason to keep me alive." King kept his stare on Brown. "But if I tell you what you want to know, then there's also no reason to keep me alive. What's in it for me?"

"Your worth as a source of information is only one consideration, as indicated by the cost-benefit analysis. Cooperation on your part, while unlikely, would necessitate modification of the analysis and alter the recommended course of action."

King very deliberately rolled his eyes. "Can we just skip the theatrics, Brown? You're not fooling anyone."

Brown cocked his head sideways. "Sigler, if I had my way, you'd be wearing fifty pounds of chain link at the bottom of the Seine."

King chuckled, but the implications of the comment were

troubling. *Were we wrong about Brown and Brainstorm being one and the same?* Then he recalled something Brainstorm had said about his being a statistical outlier: *Leaving you alive for any length of time is pushing my luck.*

Brainstorm, whether an artificial intelligence or Brown masquerading as one, dealt in probabilities. Brown had made his fortune by accurately calculating the odds and always placing a winning bet, but King had consistently defied probabilistic expectations. That had given him the winning edge in those previous encounters, and right now, it was his only advantage.

I have to do the unexpected, he thought. *That's the only way I'm getting out of this.*

"I'll tell you what, Brown. It just so happens that I've got some questions of my own that I'd like answered."

"And why on earth would I tell you anything? You're not exactly in a position to negotiate."

King smiled. "Who said anything about negotiating? You're a gambler, right? I'll play you for it. Loser answers the winner's questions, truthfully and honestly."

"This is ridiculous," Pradesh said. "We're wasting time here. We should synch the quantum device and activate the network."

King glanced over at the man. Pradesh was some kind of tech expert... Suddenly he recalled where he had heard the man's name.

During the course of Aleman's investigations into Brainstorm, King had reviewed numerous intelligence reports from the CIA's cyber-warfare division, and Bandar Pradesh had been on a short list of hackers with the skill and resources to facilitate Brainstorm's activities. Born in Kashmir India, but raised in London, he was more than just a computer geek. Utilizing the hacker alias "Shiva," Pradesh had become a sort of cyber mercenary, hiring his services out to anyone who could meet his price, a client list that featured multinational corporations and governments, including the United States. Pradesh was thought to be one of the leading programmers involved in the creation of the Stuxnet virus, which had temporarily crippled Iran's efforts at uranium enrichment.

Stuxnet, King recalled, had targeted computer systems governing the operation of power plants.

Energy again.

Brown ignored the hacker's outburst and continued to regard King from across the desktop. Brainstorm, curiously, remained quiet. Finally, the gambler shifted forward. "I'm supposed to believe that you would be truthful?"

"I could say the same," King returned. "But, for whatever it's worth, you would have my word. Scout's honor."

"I've read about you, Sigler, and I know you were never a Boy Scout."

King shrugged.

Brown fell back into silence for a moment, then stood and turned to the security guard leaning on the desk. "Give us the room."

The man's face twisted into a mask of concern. "Mr. Brown, if half of what I've heard about this guy is true..."

"He's tied up, right? Wait outside. I'll call if I need you."

The guard sighed but eased off the desk and motioned for the other man to join him.

Brown looked to Pradesh. "You, too."

The hacker made no effort to hide his stunned disbelief. "Surely you don't mean to go through with this."

Brown ignored him and settled back into his chair, and after a moment, Pradesh retreated from the room, muttering under his breath. When the door to the office opened, King could hear the noise of the casino, jazz melodies undercut with a dull roar of conversation. Then the door clicked shut, returning the room to total silence.

Brown reached into a drawer and took out a small red box

about the size of a pack of cigarettes. He opened one end and withdrew a deck of playing cards. After discarding the jokers, he began to shuffle. "I didn't take you for a gambler, Sigler. I think you may be in over your head here."

"And yet I keep beating you."

"Not this time." He placed the deck face down between them. "Blackjack, no hole cards, no splits or double-downs. One bet per game, and I'm the house, which means the decisions are yours."

Brown didn't seem to be asking for permission, so King merely nodded. Brown's rules, particularly the fact that both of King's cards would be showing, eliminated virtually every concession to the player in a game that was already stacked in favor of the house, but inasmuch as King's fate was entirely in Brown's hands, he wasn't in a position to complain.

Brown cut the deck, then looked at King. "What's your opening bet?"

King knew exactly what to offer. "Bill Downey. You seem to need him for something, so if I lose, I'll tell you where he is."

It seemed like a safe bet. If Brown's goons went looking for Downey, they'd start in the man's hotel room where King had left him, so there was nothing to be gained by holding back the knowledge. And he might just glean some insight into what Brown was really up to, and why it was so important for Downey to have one of the quantum phones.

"And if you win? What question would you like me to answer?"

"Something simple. The honest truth about Brainstorm. Admit that it's all bullshit."

A wry smile quirked the gambler's expression, then he nodded and with a flourish, expertly dealt out four cards: The five of diamonds and the nine of spades to King; the two of diamonds and the queen of hearts to himself.

"Not like I've got much choice," King muttered. "Hit me."

Brown flipped out a seven of clubs. "Twenty-one for the player."

King let out his breath in low sigh. Brown proceeded to deal a card to himself—the seven of spades for nineteen—then another—the king of clubs.

"Player wins," Brown said without a hint of disappointment. He then set the deck down and raised his eyes, meeting King's stare, but said nothing.

An electronic voice issued smoothly from the speaker on the desktop. "Touché, Mr. Sigler."

For a moment, King wasn't sure what was going on, but then a broad smile cracked Brown's inscrutable expression. "As kids today would say…Duh! Of course, Brainstorm and I are one and the same. Artificial intelligence? Seriously?"

King's elation, both from having won the hand and getting at the truth, was short-lived. "Why? How?"

"The reason why should be obvious. I was unbeatable in the casino and at the track, but I wanted more. I wanted real power. So I took my talents to the stock market, then I played the real estate game and got filthy rich. But what I could never get was respect.

"People don't respect a schmuck from Atlantic City, even when he has more money than God. No matter how much I made, I would never have been anything more than a celebrity sideshow, and that just wasn't good enough.

"I thought about creating a new personality, but then I had, if you'll pardon the pun, a brainstorm. I would hide behind a computer. People are already used to letting computers tell them what to do. We hardly ever interact with real people any more. Corporate executive boards actually like being able to blame their actions on the computers. It's a lot easier to put ten thousand people out of work when you can say you did it because the computer said it was the most efficient thing to do.

"Of course, I didn't just come right out and say that's what

I was. That would have been too obvious. It was so much better to create the impression, start some rumors, and then let everyone's imagination take care of the rest."

Brown's admission brought none of the satisfaction King had anticipated. It was so obvious, or should have been, and confirmation of the fact seemed little different from the moment a parent finally confesses the truth about Santa Claus to a child who's already figured it out. "So how'd you pull off the little ventriloquist act?"

Brown's smile broadened. "Pretty nifty trick, right? I did the risk-benefit analysis myself and entered it as text while you were unconscious. Most of it was prerecorded. The rest of it was a little more difficult. I have a foot-operated text entry interface under this desk. I've gotten pretty good at tapping out messages with my toe."

Brown slid a hand over the desk and gathered the cards from the first hand into a neat stack. "So, what shall we play for now?"

King considered the matter carefully. He wasn't a believer in luck and knew that this initial victory meant nothing in the scheme of things. He had to keep Brown talking, keep the game going until he could figure out a way to get free. "Okay, I've got it. These quantum phones of yours. What have you really got planned for them? I recognize Pradesh; he's a hacker, a cyberterrorist for hire. I doubt he has the resources to invent portable quantum computer technology, so his role in this is something else…" King thought about the rumors of Pradesh's involvement in the Stuxnet attack. Was that it? Some kind of computer attack targeting power stations, supported by quantum computing power?

Brown nodded thoughtfully. "So, if you win the next hand, I tell you what's really going on. And if I win?"

"Same stakes. I give you Downey."

Brown's smile turned hard, then he said simply, "No."

King blinked, but kept silent.

"I said you were in over your head," Brown continued. "I can tell you're no gambler, Sigler. Gambling isn't about the cards or how the dice roll. It's about the bet; what you're willing to risk and more importantly, knowing what your opponent is willing to risk. You bet that information against something that you already knew to be factual. That tells me that you consider the information about Bill Downey's location to be of little value to you. Ergo, it's of no value to me."

King felt his pulse quicken as the truth of his opponent's statement hit home. He had underestimated Brown, fallen into the very trap he'd thought to set for the other man. "All right," he said slowly. "You decide."

Brown picked up the deck as if preparing to deal. "The rest of your team. If I win, you give them up. Your plan, radio frequencies…if they're in disguise like you were, tell me who they are."

King felt a glimmer of hope but hid the reaction behind a mask of feigned outrage. "You expect me to give up my team? Sacrifice my friends? Not a chance. How about you just let me call them off, send the abort code?"

"Risk, Sigler. If you aren't willing to take a chance, then you're not ready to play this game."

"I don't have the right to gamble with other people's lives."

Brown made a dismissive gesture. "Happens all the time. You should know that better than anyone. Your Chess Team would risk their lives to take me down or learn what I'm really up to. How is this any different? But if it makes you feel any better, security is already conducting a sweep of the guests. They've probably already identified some of your team."

King narrowed his eyes, took a breath, and then nodded. "Deal."

Brown flipped the cards over with deliberate slowness, his gaze never leaving King's face.

King felt another measure of hope as he glanced down at his first card: the ace of hearts.

Brown turned over the king of spades for himself.

King was a little disappointed to see that his second card was the six of clubs. *Seven or seventeen*, he thought.

Brown's next card was the ten of hearts.

Twenty. Crap.

Without waiting for a prompt, Brown dealt King another card: Eight of diamonds. "Fifteen," he said. "You need a five to draw, six to win."

He turned over another card, glanced at it, and then deposited it in front of King. It was the queen of spades.

King sagged back in his chair.

"Luck is a fickle bitch," Brown observed coldly. "Time to settle your account, Sigler. Let's have it."

For a moment, King pondered putting the gambler on a wild goose chase—giving him bogus radio frequencies, identifying the few names he remembered from the guest list as Chess Team operators in disguise—but ultimately all that would accomplish would be to piss his foe off. Finally, he said, "The joke's on you, Brown. There is no team. Not in the field, at least."

Anger glinted in Brown's eyes. "You're lying."

"I wish I were. It would be nice to think that Bishop was waiting for my signal to bust in here and take your head off. But this was a solo op; no backup, minimum footprint."

Brown slammed the cards down on the desk. "You're lying," he repeated, his voice taut like a wire about to snap.

"I gave you my word," King persisted, not sure why it mattered. "I'm not lying to you. I would have preferred a tactical assault, but it was too risky. We knew you'd be here, exposed, so we decided to try a covert approach." He rattled off the details of the scheme, omitting only the matter of where he had left Downey. He could tell that the gambler was still unconvinced, so he added. "I would never have taken the bet if it meant actually risking the lives of my team. But I had to make you think it was important."

"It doesn't matter. I never thought you'd tell me the truth, and I don't have the time or patience to wring the truth out of you." Brown shook his head, rose to his feet and strode for the door. "But at least I will have the satisfaction of knowing that you won't be interfering with my activities again."

"One last game," King called out, craning his head around to follow the other man's progress. "For everything."

Brown stopped, but did not look back. "You don't have anything left to bet."

"No, but you do." King's mind was racing to come up with a plan. "Look at yourself. 'A schmuck from Atlantic City.' That's what you said, right? You wanted more than that, and now you've got it. You've got everything. Brainstorm practically runs the whole world, right? So why aren't you satisfied?"

King saw he had Brown's attention...*but what to do with it?*

"Because once you've won everything, what's the point? You didn't want more power, more respect. That never really mattered to you. You wanted a bigger game."

The gambler slowly turned around, still saying nothing.

"So, you're right. I might not have anything left to bet, but that's not why you play the game, is it? What do you say, Brown? Take a chance?"

"It's a very tempting proposition, Sigler." Brown blinked, then turned and opened the door. The noise of the casino briefly filled the room then was silenced as the door closed behind the two security men who now advanced, pistols already in hand.

"You've been a worthy opponent," Brown said. "But this

was only ever a momentary diversion. I'm playing a much bigger game than you can possibly imagine. And now I'm afraid your luck truly has run out."

ACTION / REACTION

14.

Paris—2015 UTC/Local

Brown circled around his desk, picking up the two phones—King's dedicated Chess Team phone and the quantum device—and casually slipped them in a pocket as he moved. King followed the gambler in his peripheral vision, but his primary focus was on the guards.

He had not expected to accomplish anything with his little game of chance. Certainly, he'd harbored no illusions that it might lead to his freedom, but even as he probed Brown for information, he'd wrestled with the matter of how to escape. Unfortunately, the plastic zip-tie binding his wrists together had not yielded a single millimeter to his surreptitious efforts, and that severely limited his options. His only chance would come when they moved him from the office to some out of the way corner of the riverboat, presumably the place where they intended to execute him, and that would mean cutting it very close.

As the two security men approached, King threw his weight to the side, toppling his chair over. He slammed onto his left shoulder, the impact driving the air from his lungs in a whoosh and sending a spike of pain through his head, but he'd done what he could to prepare himself for the crash and recovered his wits quickly.

The guards saw what he was doing and reacted without thinking, rushing forward to prevent what looked like an escape attempt, and that was exactly what King had been hoping for. Although the chair remained intact and his arms were still securely bound, one of the pair got close enough for King to wrap his nerveless fingers around the man's ankle.

The guard spat an oath as he wrenched his leg free of King's grasp.

The other man chuckled. "I told you he wouldn't go quietly."

The words were barely spoken when King twisted his body and snaked out a foot to sweep the second guard's feet out from under him. The man's arms windmilled as he landed flat on his back alongside King, and as he fell, King twisted again and kicked savagely at the man's head. Two solid strikes left the man senseless on the floor.

The first guard reacted instantly, bringing his gun around and taking aim at King's writhing form, but even as he did, something changed in his eyes. He blinked, as if unable to bring his target into focus, and then abruptly crumpled to the ground. The tetrodotoxin, administered when King had pressed his ring against the man's leg, had done its job quickly.

Brown watched in disbelief as the melee, which had lasted only a couple of seconds, abruptly ended with both of his men incapacitated, but when King began maneuvering closer to one of the fallen guards, hoping to find a knife with which to cut himself free, the gambler sprang into action. He dashed around the desk and snatched up one of the fallen pistols.

King could tell by the uncertain way Brown held the weapon that the man was unused to this sort of thing. He had built his success on manipulation and playing the probabilities, and he had always relied on hirelings to take care of the dirty work. But the gun was a Glock 17—no bothersome safety to fumble with—and with only about ten feet between them, there was little chance that Brown would miss if he pulled the trigger.

King pushed closer to the guard he had dosed with the ring, but kept his eyes on Brown. "You're probably responsible for hundreds, maybe thousands of deaths, but I'll bet you've never had to do the deed yourself," he said. "It's one thing to order someone's death, but pulling the trigger yourself? Not as easy as you thought it would be."

Now he was the one gambling, and he was betting his life on the fact that his taunts would actually make Brown stop and think—not about the consequences of shooting him, but rather about how he still possessed a small army of mercenary guards only a few minutes away, any of whom would be more than happy to dispatch King.

But then Brown's eyes hardened and his grip on the pistol steadied. A cold smile curled the corners of the gambler's mouth. "There is a ninety-nine point nine percent probability that shooting you dead will make me the happiest person in the world."

King watched, in startling detail, as Brown's finger tensed and the trigger mechanism started to move…

And then his world was filled with light and noise.

15.

Julia was relieved to learn that the museum director had indeed spoken with Carutius about closing the exhibit early. The Frenchman wasn't happy about it, but he seemed appreciative of Julia's attempts to smooth things over. "These things are out of our control, *n'est-ce pas?*"

She nodded, commiserating, but with the bureaucratic task completed, her smoldering curiosity about the underlying reason for Carutius's decision blossomed into full fire. Why on earth was Carutius running radiometric dating tests on the fragments? There was no dispute about their age, and the tests would be inconclusive anyway, revealing only the age of the materials used—which in the case of the sandstone chunks would run to millions of years—while telling nothing about when the statues themselves had been fashioned. Carutius was up to something, and Julia wanted to know what. It was, after all, part of her job description.

As she reached the corridor fronting La Chappelle gallery, she noticed a pair of figures lurking at the closed gate—a lithe woman with short, spiky hair, and a teenaged girl with jet-black hair and a swarthy Amerindian complexion. The two were dressed casually—jeans, t-shirts, sneakers—looking no different than most of the other visitors who roamed the museum's halls, but something about the urgency in their expression told Julia that they were anything but ordinary tourists.

"This exhibition is temporarily closed," she said as she approached.

Both of them turned to her, but it was the girl that spoke. "I'm looking for Mr. Carutius." Although she hesitated with the name, as if her mouth had tried to use a different word first, her tone was every bit as serious as the look on her face. "Is he in there?"

Julia peered back at them, wondering what possible business these two could have with the wealthy and influential man. She shuffled through a variety of responses but then sublimated her impulse to put them off, and instead motioned for them to follow her. The woman's face creased with concern but the girl seemed both grateful and anxious as she fell into step behind Julia.

She led them to a blank access door a few steps down the corridor from the roll-up gate, tapped in her security code and when the electronic lock disengaged, turned the knob.

"I probably shouldn't be letting you in like this," she said, but her curiosity was now burning even brighter. Maybe if Carutius was distracted with this pair, she'd be able to figure out why he had really closed the exhibit.

The corridor beyond was conspicuously bland in contrast to the public areas, but it was a short walk to another door that opened in the rear of the exhibition hall. As she reached for the doorknob, Julia became aware of a low buzzing sound, like the noise of fluorescent light fixtures, but amplified several times over, emanating from beyond. Waves of resonance vibrated through the metal skin of the door.

"That's strange," she said, glancing over her shoulder. The woman and the girl didn't seem to grasp how unusual the sound was. Shaking her head, she opened the door.

The atonal sound was considerably louder now, setting Julia's teeth on edge. A moment later she spied its source, an array of portable speakers lined up in front of the display case containing several pieces of debris from the Sakyamuni Buddha—the smaller and older of the two carvings.

Carutius stood nearby, hunched over a computer monitor, and was so completely focused on what he was doing that he failed to notice the new arrivals. Julia's attention was drawn to the table and to a bank of little plastic disks that had been positioned to face the display case. She recognized the disks from her time spent in radiometry laboratories; they were film badge dosimeters, designed to warn the wearer of exposure to a potentially lethal dose of x-ray or gamma radiation. *Surely he's not performing the dating tests here*, she thought.

"It *is* you!" The girl had to shout to be heard over the droning sound, and before Julia could think to forestall her, she dashed forward to confront Carutius. "What are you doing here?"

The big man spun around, clearly startled. Julia braced herself for the outburst to come, expecting to be the focus of his rage. She didn't care; he was up to something, and it was her duty to find out, even if it meant drawing fire from her superiors.

But the flash of anger—if it was even there to begin with—faded as soon as Carutius's gaze lit on the girl's face, replaced by equal parts recognition and alarm.

"You?" he gasped.

Julia looked anew at the teenager, wondering how it was possible that this wide-eyed American Indian girl could possibly know the European financier. When Carutius spoke again, Julia realized that whatever the explanation was, it was something beyond her wildest imaginings. It wasn't so much what he said as his grave demeanor that sent a chill down the curator's spine.

"Fiona." His ominous whisper was strangely audible despite the ambient humming. "You shouldn't be here."

16.

As soon as he heard the thunderous detonation, Timur Suvorov opened the door to the office and swept into the room in a low stance, his silenced Uzi machine pistol, an untraceable black market purchase, leading the way. The improvised flash-bang grenade he had tossed into the small room a moment before had probably incapacitated everyone inside, but he wasn't going to take any chances. He pivoted to the right, scanning the corners of the room, even as his teammate, close friend, and second-in-command, Ian Kharitonov rushed in behind him and cut to the left.

The tactical entry proved unnecessary; the four occupants lay motionless, clustered together in the center of the room. Suvorov allowed himself a satisfied smile. This was going well.

The original plan had called for a dynamic assault on the riverboat, with his small team taking out the sizable security force and then herding the rest of the passengers together in the casino. While the audacious scheme was well within the ability of his Spetsnaz team, Suvorov had felt no small measure of relief when his lookout—an SVR operative who had infiltrated the event—had radioed him with the news that the target had left the main casino and moved to an office belowdecks. Suvorov had deftly crafted a contingency that would minimize their visibility and increase their chances of success by an order of magnitude. The former consideration was particularly important; although they would be leaving a false trail that would point to the raid being the work of a criminal gang, there would nevertheless be a scrupulous investigation by the gendarmerie. There was no telling what telltale clues they might have left behind that would lead back to the Spetsnaz, the GRU and the Russian government. His encounter with Julia Preston at the Louvre for example, was just the sort of thing that could have unexpected consequences. Keeping the mayhem to a minimum would reduce some of the public demand for a comprehensive investigation into the night's events.

The original plan also would have resulted in dozens of casualties—security personnel, passengers, possibly even members of his team—and while Suvorov understood that was simply the cost of victory, he was pleased that such a level of violence would not be required. It was easy for the politicians, safe in their houses of power thousands of miles away, to say 'whatever it takes,' but it was the soldiers who had to live with the consequences. Spetsnaz training had hardened him against the emotional toll of taking lives, but there was no way to exorcise the ghosts of innocent victims lost to collateral damage.

Of course, it was much too early for self-congratulation. Locating and securing the target had been the easy part. Getting off the riverboat with their human prize would be another matter entirely. The noise of the stun grenade would almost certainly bring more security guards running. It was time to get moving.

He hastened to the center of the room and scanned the faces of the unmoving men to identify the target. The picture he had was from an old SVR file; the target had done a very good job of hiding his identity, avoiding surveillance cameras and even erasing all traces of his existence from digital archives. Still, there was enough of a similarity between the man lying before him and the grainy image in the photograph to verify that he had indeed found his prey.

Suvorov allowed himself a grim smile as he thought about the SVR and GRU interrogators in Moscow tripping over each other for the chance to get at the information in this man's head. He knelt beside the supine form, pleased to see that the man was starting to regain his senses. "Sorry to cut short your party, but it's time to go Mr. Brown."

17.

King's ears were ringing from the detonation, but he could just make out a few of the words the newcomer had spoken. *Russian*, he thought, and that bit of information was enough for him to draw an obvious conclusion. Russian commandos, probably a Spetsnaz team—Russian Special Forces, arguably the deadliest unconventional fighting men on Earth—wanted Brown as badly as he did.

The flash-bang had gone off behind him, sparing his eyes from the blinding brilliance of the flash, but the concurrent shock wave had nonetheless left him disoriented and faintly queasy. He remained motionless as the two black-clad commandos hauled their captive erect and hurried from the office, but as soon as they were gone, he resumed his efforts at getting free.

Filled with a new sense of urgency, he twisted his torso back and forth until, with a satisfying crack, the chair to which he had been bound splintered apart. The intensity of his struggle also proved too much for the thin plastic strap that held his wrists together; the zip-tie, designed for nothing more strenuous than securing electrical wires and computer cables, broke apart, and suddenly he was free.

A throb of pain accompanied the return of normal circulation to his freed extremities. Blood immediately began oozing from ragged welts on both wrists where the plastic tie had cut deep into his skin, but he ignored the wounds, getting to his feet and lingering in the room only long enough to snatch up the Glock that Brown had dropped when the flash-bang had gone off.

He edged past the open door into the hallway beyond, ready to duck back into the office at the first sign of trouble. The noise from the casino, just barely audible through the lingering effects of the flash-bang to his auditory system, was different now. No music now, just a dull roar of confusion. The partygoers had heard the sound of the stun grenade explosion, and King didn't doubt that a gaggle of steroid-crazed Alpha Dog security men were already rushing down to investigate. For the moment however, the corridor was empty. With the Glock at the ready, he advanced at a jog and headed away from the source of the tumult, toward what he hoped was the path the Russians had followed.

Russians, he thought again, scowling as he ran. In the feverish quest to unmask Brainstorm, it hadn't occurred to anyone that there might be other interested parties. That should have been obvious really; the Brainstorm network was global in nature, as were Brown's schemes for world domination. Unfortunately, Brown's capture would not mean the end of either. Now the Russians would control Brainstorm, with full access to Brown's incredible mental abilities, his extensive network of operatives, and worst of all, the ability to execute the gambler's audacious plans. King saw only two ways to stop that from happening; he either had to save Brown from the Russians or kill the man.

A door at the end of the corridor opened onto a narrow

flight of stairs, which in turn led him onto the open foredeck of the riverboat. At each blind corner, King paused just long enough to make sure that he wasn't about to run headlong into an ambush. As he emerged from the stairwell, his caution paid off.

He had barely peeked around the doorpost, exposing only a sliver of his body, when the bulkhead to his left exploded in a spray of wood and fiberglass splinters. King ducked back, but did not allow the knowledge of the danger ahead to mire him in inertia. He thrust the Glock into the open, squeezing off two quick shots, and then immediately somersaulted through the opening. As he came out of the combat roll, he immediately got the pistol up and started a visual sweep for the location of the shooter.

Nothing.

With each second that ticked by, each thump of his heart in his chest, the danger multiplied. He was out in the open, completely visible to a gunman who still remained invisible to him. But no shots came. The gunman had already moved on.

Not good, King thought. He rose from cover and hastened to the railing that ringed the perimeter of the deck.

The dark water of the Seine lapped against the low hull of the riverboat only a few feet away. In the darkness, hidden from the glare of the deck lights by the shadow of the railing, it was hard to distinguish the oblong outline of a boat. It looked like a semi-rigid inflatable Zodiac, though it was impossible to tell since the hull was black, the same color as the clothes worn by its two occupants. One man was just settling in at the prow, his right hand still gripping a compact machine pistol. His comrade sat at the stern, tending an idling outboard motor. In the instant that King's eyes registered this fact, the man twisted the throttle control and the motor roared to life, the screws throwing up a froth of spray, stark white and glittering against the inky surface of the still river.

King didn't even pause to think about what to do next. In a fluid motion, he planted his left hand on the rail and vaulted out into the night.

18.

As King's feet hit the hard fiberglass deck, the boat lurched forward, the thrust of the outboard's screws finally overcoming the craft's inertia. King pitched backward, stumbling over a low aluminum bench seat, and crashed into the man seated at stern. Their combined weight and the sudden forward thrust nearly sent both men into the river, but the commando managed to wrap his arms around the engine cowling to arrest his fall, and King knotted his fingers in the man's dark combat uniform to prevent his own.

That was all the help he got from the commando. The man freed one of his arms and immediately started pummeling King with his fist. The strikes were awkward, seemingly desperate, but the rapid impacts sent bursts of pain through King's skull, further disorienting him and for a moment, all he could think about was holding on tighter. The assault abruptly relented and King felt the man shift in his grasp, trying for a better angle of attack. The next wave of blows would, he knew, be far more decisive.

Setting his jaw in anticipation of the pain he knew was coming, King pulled the man in close and thrust his torso up, ramming his forehead into the commando's chin. Light exploded across his vision as he made contact, but even over the roar of the outboard, the satisfying crunch of the commando's jaw breaking was audible. The Russian slumped in King's grasp, his hold on the engine cowling slipping away, and he teetered back over the gunwale. King released his grip and pushed the man away, hastening the latter's plunge into the Seine.

There was no time to savor the victory. King twisted around to find the second commando looming above him. Clad in black from head to toe, the man was almost invisible against the backdrop of night, but King had no difficulty making out the glinting steel of the knife in the man's right hand as it slashed down toward him. He shrank away, pressing himself into the bilge space, but there was nowhere to go.

The knife slashed again but even as he felt its tip snag the fabric of his dinner jacket, King brought his own right arm up and caught the man's forearm in the crook of his elbow. The commando reflexively tried to pull away, but King trapped his foe's forearm with the heel of his left hand and then with a savage scissor-action, broke the man's wrist. The commando howled in pain; the knife fell from his fingers and clattered into the bilge space. King, still on his back, did not release his hold on the injured limb, but drew his knees up, planted his feet squarely in his opponent's chest, and used his legs to launch the man out into the river.

In the moment that followed, King wanted nothing more than to simply lay still and savor a few seconds where no one wanted to kill him, but he knew that, despite this initial victory, his real objective was slipping further away with every tick of the clock.

He rolled over and struggled to get to his hands and knees. The cramped bilge space at the rear of the boat conspired with the undulations of the craft as if bumped across wakes and ripples in the river's surface to make it a ridiculously complicated task. He finally managed to grasp the control lever on the outboard and hauled himself into a sitting position.

The inflatable boat was moving at an almost perpendicular angle away from the floating casino. He could make out the city skyline in every direction, but everything in the foreground was shrouded in darkness. As his eyes adjusted to the low light, he could make out the ripples left by the wake of another craft. It was moving away in the same general direction he was now traveling, and he followed the ripples to their source: two more Zodiacs, barely more than shadows, a few hundred yards away, just passing under one of the many bridges that spanned the river and connected the city proper with Île Saint-Louis. He adjusted the tiller to bring his boat into line behind them and opened the throttle wide. The bow of the craft came up as the burst of speed sent it rocketing forward, almost skimming across the surface of the Seine.

He could tell he was closing the gap on the retreating boats. If their operators were the professionals he guessed them to be, they would sacrifice speed for stealth. Unfortunately, that meant they would notice his approach, and if they didn't already know that he had commandeered one of their boats and reduced their fighting force by two, they would at the very least be alerted to the fact that something was wrong.

He took stock of his tactical situation. The Glock he had taken from Brown was gone. There was no sign of the pistol in the bilge space, and he could only assume that it had gone into the river during the struggle with the commandos. His foes had likewise taken their guns with them into the Seine. The only weapon available to him was the knife that the second man had dropped. King retrieved the blade and gave it a cursory examination.

In the darkness, it was difficult to distinguish any manufacturing marks, but his fingertips probed the knurled metal of the cylindrical hilt—heavier than expected, making for a poorly balanced weapon—and the odd shape of the finger guard, which sported a metallic stud that reminded King of a gun's magazine release button. It was, he realized, a ballistic knife. Depressing the stud would trigger a blast of pressurized gas inside the hilt and simultaneously release a mechanism holding the blade in place, subsequently launching the blade like a crossbow bolt.

When he recognized the weapon, any remaining doubts about the identity of the commando team were swept away. The ballistic knife was the signature weapon of the *voyska spetsialnogo naznacheniya*, the elite special forces of Russia's military intelligence directorate, the *Glavnoye Razvedyvatel'noye Upravleniye.*

If there was a Russian equivalent of Chess Team, it was the GRU Spetsnaz.

King knew the outcome of his first battle with the Russian commandos had been more a matter of luck than anything else, and as Brown had pointed out, luck was fickle.

He backed off the throttle a little, somewhat reducing the noise and fury of his progress across the watercourse. The longer he succeeded in not attracting the attention of the occupants of the other boats, the better his chances of surviving the next encounter. For that reason, he also pulled the lapels of his dinner jacket together, covering up the white shirt beneath, and sank down low, trying to hide as much of his face from view as he could.

He risked a quick glance over the bow. The nearest Zodiac was now only about a hundred yards away, the other at least fifty yards beyond that. If they were operating as he expected, Brown would be in the closer boat, with the lead craft acting as a vanguard to make sure that the landing zone was secure. That would work to his advantage; he would only need to subdue Brown's immediate captors, and with a little luck, the men in the front boat would never even know that their comrades were in trouble.

There was that word again. *Luck.*

19.

Fiona ignored the big man's dire pronouncement. "What are you doing here?" she demanded, her fists on her hips in a defiant pose.

The man she knew as Hercules and Alexander Diotrophes —the man now calling himself Carutius—ignored her and turned his gaze to the woman that had guided Fiona and Sara into the exhibit hall. "Dr. Preston, I need you to take them out of here immediately."

The woman blinked at him and for a moment, seemingly on the verge of complying, but then Sara stepped forward. "Just a damn minute. Fiona asked you a question, and I think we all deserve an answer. I've heard a lot about you... Frankly, I think a lot of it is bullshit, but one thing I do know is that you're a magnet for trouble."

A gleam that might have been humor flickered in the man's eyes. "And here you are, Sara. Interesting."

"Are you following us?" Fiona asked.

"Not everything in the world revolves around you, my dear. The fact of the matter is that your presence here is a complication, and one that I wish to immediately resolve.

Thus…" He glanced at Dr. Preston again. "My insistence that you leave immediately."

"The pictures are singing to me," Fiona blurted. "When I look at them…at the artwork here…it's like I can hear voices."

Alexander's brow creased as he pondered this, and Fiona realized that maybe the big man didn't have all the answers after all. Then his visage hardened again. "This changes nothing. You need to leave. You shouldn't be here. You shouldn't even be in Paris, but there's nothing to be done about that. Dr. Preston— Julia—please do as I asked. Escort them to the front gate and put them in a taxi. Get them out of here."

Julia shook her head, overcoming her paralysis. "I don't think so. This is all too much. First you close the exhibit and give me some cock-and-bull story about radiometric dating. Now these two show up and this girl says…what? That she can *hear* the paintings singing to her? And you don't even bat an eye? What the hell is going on here?"

Alexander drew a deep breath, clearly struggling to control his anger. If he wanted, the big man could probably have scooped them all up under one mighty arm and bodily carried them out the door, but Fiona resolved that she wouldn't be leaving any other way. It seemed that Sara and Julia were of the same mind, and Alexander evidently realized this. He faced Julia. "This young woman possesses a remarkable gift. She is quite possibly the last person alive with knowledge—albeit incomplete—of what might be the original language."

A flicker of skepticism crossed Julia's face. She glanced at Fiona, but said nothing.

"As you no doubt have learned in your own studies of anthropology, language and culture are learned behaviors, but at their heart, they represent the desire of our species to assign meaning to the physical universe. The same is true of art. In fact, artistic representations are the most basic form of communication; even before written language, people communicated with pictures. There are charcoal drawings on the walls of the Chauvet Cave made 30,000 years ago. We can't know what words those ancient peoples used to speak with one another, but we have no difficulty understanding the message in those drawings. Art and language are therefore inextricably linked, so it comes as no surprise that Fiona here would grasp this connection in a way that remains hidden to the rest of us."

"But...singing to her?"

Alexander turned his gaze to girl. "Do you literally hear singing?"

"Not exactly," Fiona equivocated. "It's like that, but...I don't know how else to describe it."

"When a person discerns a pattern, such as a mathematical regression," Alexander said, "it changes their perspective. You start to see that pattern everywhere, without even trying. This is no different."

"That makes sense," Sara said, directing her words to Fiona. "Your brain just doesn't know how to interpret the message."

He sighed and folded his arms across his chest. "That is the only answer I can give you. Now, will you leave?"

Fiona felt Sara take her hand, gently but nonetheless insistently urging her to comply with the request. Julia still appeared troubled by all that had transpired and by the lack of any real answers, but likewise seemed eager to leave the big man's daunting presence.

"Just tell me this," Fiona persisted. "Why now?"

"What do you mean?"

"This just started happening when I came in the museum. It's been months since..." She nodded meaningfully toward Julia. "That thing happened, and nothing. But the minute I set foot in the museum, it started. And there's something else. It only happens when I look at the original art. I don't feel anything when I look at photographs of the art."

"From those? Nothing." She pointed at the elaborate holograms of the Buddhas and shook her head. "But when I look at those—" Her finger moved to the display cases which seemed to contain only chunks of rock. "It's like they're screaming at me."

Alexander's eyes widened, transforming his countenance into what, on any other man, would have been a mask of outright terror. He knelt before Fiona, the top of his head still slightly higher than her own, and gripped her shoulders in either hand. "Tell me, child. What are they saying?"

20.

It took several minutes for King to get within fifty yards of the nearest Zodiac, but his cautious approach evidently worked. There was no indication that the Spetsnaz men were aware that anything was amiss. He risked another quick glance and saw three figures—two of them merely black silhouettes, but the third revealing uncovered pale skin, silvery hair, and a white formal shirt that were all in stark contrast to the surrounding darkness.

King ducked back down, made a final course correction and opened the throttle wide. The noise of the engine revving at full power would carry across the water, alerting the commandoes to his approach, but at maximum speed, his boat would close the distance in a matter of seconds, hopefully before his foes realized the last boat no longer contained their comrades.

The bow rose with the sudden acceleration and the boat once more seemed to skim across the river's surface, bouncing a few inches into the air each time it encountered a ripple from the wake of the preceding Zodiacs. King kept his head down and watched the frothy line of whitewater thrown up by his prey spreading out in either direction from the source in an inverted V, using it to guide him onward. As he got closer, the V all but disappeared and the chop from the other boat's wake hammered through the fiberglass hull.

He gripped the ballistic knife in his right fist, and braced his feet against the back of the bench seat.

Right about…now.

There was a sickening crunch as the front end of King's Zodiac collided with the stern of the other craft. Had he not been anticipating the crash, the sudden stop would have catapulted King headlong, but instead he absorbed the impact with his legs, bent his knees and kept his body low in the bilge space. The nose of King's boat rode up and over the other boat's engine cowling, and then with a lurch it tilted to the right. The Zodiac hung precariously from one side of the other boat, its outboard whining loudly as the exposed screws chopped only air.

King launched into motion, rolled over the upraised gunwale of his boat and dropped down into the other.

He caught a glimpse of a commando at the bow clutching frantically at the inflatable hull in an effort to avoid being thrown into the river. King pounced on the Spetsnaz operator, planting a knee in the man's ribs. The commando's breath left him in a whoosh, as did his ability to offer any resistance when King summarily heaved him over the side of the boat.

King whirled, ready to meet the expected attack from the remaining Russian, but instead he found himself facing the silver-haired form of Graham Brown.

In deciding to ram the escaping Zodiac, King had judged the possibility that he might injure or kill Brown as an acceptable risk; in fact, Brown's fate was his single overriding concern. His mission had been to bring Brown back alive, but killing him was certainly preferable to letting the Russians have him or otherwise allowing him to escape. Brown however seemed to have come through the collision unscathed, a fact that King found strangely unsatisfying.

Brown squinted at him, trying to pierce the veil of darkness, and a look of recognition dawned. This wasn't one of his hired guns come to rescue him but his mortal enemy.

King saw Brown's hand dart into the pocket of his jacket and pull out something that reflected glints of the distant city lights—not a pistol or any other weapon, but something with the potential to be just as dangerous.

A cell phone. Not just any cell phone, but one of the quantum devices.

As King scrambled toward Brown, the latter held the phone close to his face and pressed a button. The gambler's face lit up in the glow of the device.

King tried to snatch the phone away before Brown could press any more buttons, but even as he stretched out his left hand, something slammed into his chest, knocking him back into the bow.

A dark shape had emerged from beneath the bulk of King's Zodiac: the second Spetsnaz commando.

King slashed at the man with the knife, but he was off balance, falling backward even as he tried to strike, and the man not only adroitly dodged the attack but managed a counterattack in the form of a rigid, open-handed chop to King's forearm. King's hand went instantly numb and his grip on the knife started to loosen. He clapped his free hand around his right fist, squeezing the deadened fingers tight, even as he reversed direction and tried to drive his attacker away with a backslash.

Once again, the Spetsnaz effortlessly evaded the attack, then he seized King's wrists, twisting the knife around so that its tip was poised directly above King's face. King couldn't actually see the blade in the darkness, but he knew from the position of his hands that the blade was mere inches away. Something hard struck King's abdomen, not a directed blow but a heavy object—the man's gun, dangling from a nylon web sling. King ignored the bruising impact and focused all his energy into resisting the insistent pressure driving the knife-point toward his eye. His opponent was powerful, with gravity working in the Spetsnaz's favor. The man put his full weight behind the attack, forcing the knife closer by degrees. A desperate survival instinct gave King the strength to forestall the attack but little else. The Spetsnaz had all the advantages.

And then King felt the man's fingers moving, creeping toward the stud on the hilt.

21.

Mobile device detected. Do you wish to synch? Y/N

Graham Brown felt a moment of uncertainty.

He was only peripherally aware of the life and death struggle going on a few feet away. It didn't really matter which man survived—King or his mysterious abductor—since both intended the same fate for him. He might not get another chance to do this.

He thought about Pradesh's earlier exhortation and recalled his own counter-argument. The probability of success would be drastically diminished if he did this. All his carefully laid plans were contingent upon the quantum devices being utilized in a specific manner. A deviation would have unpredictable results.

But wasn't that the true nature of gambling? Wasn't that the very thing that had motivated him to embrace this plan in the first place? Bold risks, uncertain outcomes…a final grand game of chance that would put his unique abilities to the ultimate test.

King had been more right that he would ever know.

Brown had indeed won the game, won every game. He had played so expertly that there was no longer any satisfaction at all in the victory.

Maybe it's better this way, he thought, and tapped the "Y" on the screen.

22.

Endgame HQ, Pinckney New Hampshire
2027 UTC/ 1527 Local

Lewis Aleman jiggled the empty can of Red Bull energy drink, shaking the last few drops of the beverage into his mouth, and tossed the aluminum container into a wastebasket where it rattled hollowly off several other discards.

"You should probably switch to water," Deep Blue advised from his position at an adjoining workstation. "Any more of that stuff and you'll give yourself an aneurism."

"I'd rather switch to Sam Adams," Aleman meant it only in jest. He wouldn't dream of consuming alcohol in the middle of an operation, with an agent in the field. "Why hasn't he checked in?"

"It could take a while for him to isolate Brown." Deep Blue's reply lacked confidence, and Aleman knew his superior wasn't any more satisfied with the explanation than he was.

"He could be in trouble."

"King's a big boy."

As if to punctuate the discussion, Aleman's computer monitor blinked awake as did the large plasma screen on the wall. Aleman sat up straight. "His phone is active. He's checking in."

To his dismay however, the screen displayed the words:

Login failed. Please enter a valid access code (2 attempts remaining).

"What the hell?" Something was wrong. He glanced at Deep Blue who looked equally concerned.

"King's phone uses biometric security," Deep Blue said, the question implicit.

Aleman nodded. The device, his own design, needed only a thumbprint scan—very useful for both preventing unauthorized use and rapid access in the field. There was no password or access code. Then, as lines of machine language began filling the screen, Aleman realized what he was seeing.

"That's not King's phone," he gasped. "We're being hacked."

Override accepted.

Impossible. No one in the world could hack through the layers of firewall protection he had built to protect the Chess Team mainframe. Even with the power of a device like the supercomputer used by the NSA's Echelon program, such an attack would have taken hours…days even.

Aleman was up and moving in a heartbeat, dashing across the room to a console that contained only a single, red button. Without even a moment's hesitation, he slammed his palm down on the killswitch.

Lines of code continued to flash across the plasma screen. The hacker had anticipated this action and evidently disabled the killswitch remotely. That left only one option…if it wasn't already too late. He pivoted and headed for the door.

"Aleman," Deep Blue barked. "What in God's name is happening?"

"Someone is in our system."

"Shut it down!"

"I can't. They've locked me out of the hardware."

"Then pull the goddamn plug."

"That's what I'm going to do." His profound respect for Chess Team's leader compelled the tech expert to delay a moment longer. "But the only way to do that is to destroy the mainframe. A couple incendiary grenades should do the trick. But we'll be completely cut off."

Deep Blue's eyes widened as the gravity of this revelation hit home. Chess Team's effectiveness owed no small part to their access to information and instantaneous communication. The fire suppression system would probably prevent the destruction of the entire facility—probably—but immolating the computer mainframe would be a severe blow in the long term. In the short term, it would mean hanging King out to dry. But what choice was there?

"Do it."

23.

Paris—2027 UTC

Bandar Pradesh straightened in his chair as the message on the display monitor changed. The tenth and final quantum device had been activated and was synching. A progress bar indicated that the process was nearly complete. It was taking longer than the others had, but the difference would be measured only in seconds. The quantum network was, without question, the fastest and most powerful computer on the planet. With nine nodes already active, its stutter-logic artificial intelligence could almost instantly adapt to any security protocols. The time lag was almost certainly due to the volume of information the system was downloading from the parallel network, which evidently was larger than any of the others had been.

He sighed in relief. Brown's reluctance to simply activate the tenth device hadn't been merely an aggravation. It had threatened the success of Pradesh's true agenda. He had been tempted to simply take the device and perform the final synchronization himself, but doing so might have tipped his hand at the most critical moment. In the end, he had decided to tolerate Brown's dismissal, awaiting a better opportunity to act.

He'd heard some loud noises earlier—gunshots?—no doubt Brown dealing with a captive, but he'd thought better of leaving the safety of the control room. Now he was glad for his restraint.

The progress bar jumped to 100%. The device was now synchronized and the network was active.

Adrenaline stirred in his veins and with trembling fingers, he tapped a command into the prompt:

```
>>>Awakening.exe
```

24.

King wrenched his head sideways and let the Spetsnaz drive the point of the blade down. The knife pierced through the air where his face had been an instant earlier and punched deep into the fiberglass deck. Almost simultaneously, the Russian's finger depressed the release stud on the hilt.

The knife handle went cold in King's grasp as the compressed carbon dioxide charge expanded inside the tube, but because the blade wasn't going anywhere, the blast instead blew the hilt, along with the four hands gripping it, straight up like a piston into the Russian's face.

Even as the Spetsnaz winced from the impact, King released his grip on the hilt and fumbled for the heavy object that had pounded him earlier—the Russian's gun. His fingers found the cool metal frame and recognized it instantly—an Israeli-produced Uzi 9-millimeter machine pistol, outfitted with a noise suppressor. His hand curled around the grip, depressing the safety mechanism, and in a single decisive motion, he jabbed the extended barrel up into the Russian's abdomen and pulled the trigger.

Hot brass cascaded from the ejection port, but there was

hardly any noise or recoil as the magazine emptied into the Russian's torso. King felt the man lurch as the rounds punched through him, but even before the bolt blew back on the last chamber, the Russian slumped atop him, dead or very nearly so.

King heaved the corpse away, his hands now slick with the man's blood. His eyes caught the glow of a cell phone, its light illuminating Brown's face. The gambler seemed oblivious to everything else, his attention consumed by whatever was being displayed on the screen. King snatched the device from the other man's grasp. It was the quantum phone. The small screen showed just two words:

Operation complete.

He grabbed Brown's shirtfront with his free hand and pulled the man close. "What did you just do?"

The gambler's defiant smile was particularly creepy in the phone's glow. "Locked in my bet. Nothing you can do about it now."

"We'll see about that," King growled. He punched Brown squarely on the chin, the slim phone in his hand adding just a little bit of heft to the blow, and the man slumped unconscious onto the deck.

King dropped the quantum phone into his pocket, then bent over Brown and rifled through the man's clothes to find the Chess Team phone. He was dismayed to see that it was also radiating light; somehow, Brown had activated it. He swiped his thumb over the screen and spoke the voice command that would put him in touch with Deep Blue back at headquarters.

As he waited for the call to connect, he retrieved the Uzi from the fallen commando. A quick search yielded half a dozen magazines of 9 mm rounds for the gun, a satchel full of improvised explosives—flashbangs and claymores, along with loose packets of plastique and blasting caps, and another ballistic knife. He then hauled Brown's unresisting form into the Zodiac he'd originally commandeered and climbed in after, shoving off from the damaged boat. He didn't see the third boat anywhere, but the apparent absence of the remaining members of the Spetsnaz team did not fill him with confidence. They were out there somewhere. It was only a matter of time before they realized what he had done. As he aimed the prow of the inflatable craft toward the nearest land—Île de la Cité—he heard a familiar voice in his ear.

"King!" Deep Blue sounded more frantic than King could recall ever hearing. "What's happening? Wait…"

King could just make out the words that followed over the whine of the outboard. "Aleman. Abort. I've got King on the line."

Abort? What's going on?

The voice returned to full strength. "All right, King. Report. And make it quick. We've got a shitstorm brewing here."

King did not immediately answer. He thought about the quantum phone…about how his own phone had been active when he'd taken it from Brown… "I think maybe your problems are related to mine," he said finally.

He hastily recounted what had happened on the riverboat. Aleman joined the conversation, peppering him with questions he couldn't answer when the subject of the quantum computer devices were brought up. He didn't go into detail about the game he had played, and ultimately lost, with Brown, but instead focused on Pradesh.

"Shiva?" Aleman said, using Pradesh's hacker alias. "That explains what happened here. In fact, it's the only explanation."

The tech expert quickly related the details of the cyber-attack, which had inexplicably ended only a few seconds before King had called, and just before he'd pulled the pin on a handful of incendiary grenades that would have reduced the Chess Team mainframe to a puddle of molten goo. The virtual damage was already done; there was now nothing to be gained by physically destroying the mainframe.

"With a quantum computer at his disposal, Shiva could break into any computer, anywhere. Government computers, banks...he'd control everything."

"I'm not sure that's Brown's plan," King countered. "Think about what we already know. Brown tried to develop an alternative energy source with Bluelight. Then he hosts a conference about the future of energy. And now we know he hired one of the architects of the Stuxnet computer virus to help him design the ultimate computer. What does that add up to?"

There was silence on the line, so King laid out his conclusion. "I think Brown wants control of the power grid. I think he plans to use the quantum computer to put Stuxnet into the computers controlling the grid.

"He was very insistent about making sure that the quantum computers went to ten men, all of them operations managers at big power stations. The power grid is designed so that if one station goes down, the demand can be met by others, but if you could knock out several of them simultaneously, the whole system would crash. I think Brown plans to use that threat to hold the world's electrical supply hostage." A light bulb flashed on in his head. "Or maybe he wants to destroy the grid so he can step forward with Bluelight, a power supply that doesn't require the grid."

"There's a problem with that," Aleman said. "Stuxnet is sophisticated, but it capitalizes on what are called 'day-zero' vulnerabilities. In other words, it exploits weaknesses that are built into the original programming language."

"Then he's using a different virus," King said.

"You're missing the point. Someone like Shiva wouldn't need a quantum computer to pull off what you're suggesting. Heaven knows, the power grid is vulnerable enough as it is."

That stopped King. "You're saying it would be like trying

to drive a nail with a sledge-hammer?"

"More like with a jackhammer. There's something more going on here."

"I've got one of the quantum phones with me. Maybe we can use it to reverse engineer their system and find a back door. And I've got Brown." King glanced over at the form of his nemesis. Willingly or not, the gambler was going to answer all their questions.

Suddenly a squeal of static filled his ear and he jerked the phone away as if it had stung him. The screen now read:

Connection lost

He waited a moment to see if the problem would resolve itself but there was no change. On an impulse, he took out the quantum phone but its display was dark.

He returned both phones to his pocket and focused on the immediate task of piloting the boat. The wheels of Brown's plan were now turning, he was sure of that, but where they were rolling was anyone's guess and time was running out.

25.

The cold water was more of shock to Timur Suvorov's body than the surprise attack that had preceded his plunge into the river. He remembered that Kharitonov had called out to him, warning that something was wrong, but before he could grasp what was happening, another boat had crashed into them and the next thing he knew, he was sinking into the Seine.

Sinking!

He clawed at the water, trying to swim back to the surface, but the weight of his equipment was bearing him into the murky depths like an anchor. He frantically pulled the sling of his Uzi off his shoulder, and then struggled out of the vest containing his spare magazines and an array of improvised grenades. His sodden clothes and boots still felt like an over-garment of concrete, but he was a strong swimmer and his powerful strokes reversed his journey. Nevertheless, his lungs burned with the acid of trapped carbon dioxide. The dark surface seemed impossibly far away...

He broke through with a splash, not caring if doing so re-vealed his presence to the enemy that had unexpectedly gotten the better of him, and sucked in air greedily.

He was treading water, turning slowly until he spied the barely visible silhouette of a Zodiac, evidently derelict, drifting a few yards away. The sound of a distant outboard motor drifted across the surface of the river but otherwise all was still. He swam over to the abandoned boat, and with no little difficulty, heaved himself up onto the inflated rubber hull.

The smell of fresh blood and recent death hung in the air. His probing hands found a body, wearing an outfit identical to his own. A wave of fear and anger built in his chest as he tore off the black balaclava to reveal the man's pale face and light brown hair. Suvorov burst forth in a howl of pain when he recognized the man; his teammate, his brother in every sense but the literal, Ian Kharitonov was dead.

Suvorov peered out across the river and spied the outline of another boat, the still visible wake leading almost directly back to the place where he had surfaced. Kharitonov's killer—probably one of Brown's mercenaries—was on that boat and so also, he assumed, was Brown. He mastered his emotions, forcing them down and corking them with a promise.

He couldn't bring Kharitonov back. All he could do was see the mission through, and hope for a chance to give his friend's death some meaning.

26.

"What are they saying?" Alexander repeated.

Fiona gaped at Alexander. Yet, even if the intensity of his expression and the barely subdued violence of his hold on her shoulders had not left her speechless, she would have been hard pressed to answer his question. She was faintly aware that Sara had moved close, hugging protectively, seemingly trying to pull her away from the big man's grasp, but Fiona did not move.

She didn't know how to begin describing what she felt when she looked at the pieces of stone in the display cases. It was different than with the artwork. The paintings and sculptures seemed to both sing and glow, and while she couldn't quite put that into words—into English words at least—she was starting to feel like she understood. It was like trying to describe a color; there were no words for it, you just had to find an example. She understood that the pieces of rubble had once been art, but whatever message they contained, ought to have been destroyed when the original statues had been blown up. The message of art wasn't an intrinsic thing; a message written on a piece of paper didn't fundamentally alter the paper.

Or did it?

Maybe it was like with a computer hard drive, where no matter how hard you tried to erase old data, there were always ways to retrieve the files. At least that was how it worked in all the police shows she watched on television.

Maybe what she was looking at was the original message, but all distorted and jumbled.

She was still trying to figure out how to put that idea into words when a hideous shriek ripped through the room, overpowering the atonal hum from the speakers. She clamped her hands to her ears, but the sound was undiminished, vibrating through every fiber of her body. Behind Fiona, Sara had collapsed on the floor, writhing in agony under the sonic assault that was playing havoc with her sensory disorder.

Alexander whirled to look at his equipment, undisguised concern on his face, then turned back. "Get out of here! Now!"

Fiona didn't need to be told again. She knelt beside Sara and tried to help her to her feet, aided by an uncomprehending Julia. The electronically amplified shriek changed pitch, cycling randomly through different frequencies and occasionally falling silent, but even when she heard nothing, Fiona could sense that the sounds were still present, albeit at a range inaudible to the ordinary human ear.

Then, with an almost painful abruptness, true silence came.

Sara, now on her feet and braced between Julia and Fiona, gave a tortured gasp but seemed to regain some of her strength.

Julia, sensing that her assistance was no longer required, relaxed her grip and turned to Alexander, who was now hunched over a laptop on the table. The curator hastened to confront him, but whatever demand she had been about to make died on her lips when she reached the big man's side. Her gaze was riveted to something on the table and after a moment, she reached out and plucked up one of the plastic disks. Even from halfway across the room, Fiona could see that something had changed; the center of the disk was now almost black.

"What does this mean?" Julia asked, thrusting the dosimeter into Alexander's face, her voice trembling with fear.

The big man's expression tightened, as if trying to hold back unimaginable grief. "You know what it means. We've all been exposed to a concentration of gamma radiation." He took a breath. "A lethal concentration."

The pronouncement was too mind-boggling for Fiona to process. Radiation? Lethal? That just didn't make any sense.

"Gamma rays?" Julia countered, her voice edging on hysteria. "From what?"

Alexander's reply, if he had intended one, never came, for in the next instant, the room heaved and Fiona felt herself falling sideways into oblivion.

CAUSE / BECAUSE

In the beginning, there was everything.

From the first moment of existence, the first moment of time, the universe was complete.

Before that instant…there was no before. Time did not exist. Nothing existed. And then, the singularity…what scientists would some fourteen billion years later call 'the Big Bang,' brought everything into being.

All of the matter and energy that would ever exist began at that moment, as did the laws and forces that would govern their behavior. And because those laws were immutable, the very nature of reality and the ultimate destiny of this new universe existed as well. There was no other possible outcome. Everything that would happen—the changing states of matter and energy, the creation of simple elements from subatomic particles, the forging of the primary elements by gravity and atomic fusion and violent supernovae explosions into more complex metals, the emergence of molecules, even the arrangement of those molecules into living organisms—all of it was, from that incipient moment, inevitable. Everything that would ever exist, existed in that moment as an eventuality.

The final eventuality, where all that had been brought into being would return to the singularity, where even time and concepts such as before and after would cease to have meaning—the thing that Kushan villagers in the Bamiyan Valley had, with astonishing insight, imagined to be Angra Mainyu, *demon of darkness and bringer of absolute destruction—had always existed as well, poised like the Sword of Damocles above all that had been made reality in the instant of the singularity.*

But this awakening…this was something different.

27.

King guided the Zodiac north, up the channel separating the two islands, and scanned the banks looking for a place to land the boat. He had just spied a stone ramp, descending from the battlement-like seawall surrounding Île de la Cité, when the hull beneath him began to shudder as if passing over a washboard. King eased back on the throttle, letting the boat coast, but if anything, the turbulence seemed to increase. The black water all around him rippled violently, sloshing onto the nearby ramp and splashing in frothy waves against the seawall. Huge stone blocks were tumbling from the wall, crashing onto the nearby ramp and splashing into the undulating surface of the river.

King killed the outboard, and as the throaty roar died away, the night became filled with a discordant symphony of car alarms and grinding stone, punctuated every few seconds by an explosion. Even from his low vantage, King could see city lights bobbing crazily. Far off in the distance, a brilliantly illuminated needle shape—the Eiffel Tower—was snapping back and forth like the radio antenna of a speeding car.

"Earthquake?" King muttered. Paris was one of the most

geologically stable places in Europe, but impossible as it was, there could be no other explanation.

The shaking continued, intensifying, and the cacophony grew louder. Then, as abruptly as a candle flame being blown out by a stiff wind, the entire skyline went dark. Other lights started to dance across the skyline, not stationary fixtures but the running lights of aircraft—helicopters, he guessed— spiraling chaotically downward to disappear in the darkened cityscape.

King shuddered in horrified disbelief. Helicopters were falling from the sky. An earthquake couldn't cause that. *What the hell is happening?*

As suddenly as it had begun, the earthquake stopped. The deep rumbling noise ceased, but the din of the temblor's aftermath continued to fill the lightless city—strident alarms and screams, punctuated by the crump of distant explosions and collapsing buildings. Though he could barely comprehend it, he knew that in a few mere seconds, the City of Light had become a disaster zone.

Brown still lay unmoving in the boat, and King dismissed the idea of trying to rouse him. The gambler was unlikely to share anything meaningful and King wasn't in the mood to entertain the man's triumphant crowing. He knew that this event was somehow connected to the activation of the quantum phone, and his gut told him that Brown's grand scheme would not merely be limited to a regional catastrophe. Whatever his plan, this was surely only the opening gambit.

There was one man who would be able to give King the information he needed. Not Brown. From past experience, King knew the gambler rarely troubled himself with the details—the physical realities—of his schemes. No, the man who could answer his questions was the man who had built the quantum phones in the first place.

King fired up the outboard, and brought the boat around, heading back toward the floating casino and the man who had taken his *nom de guerre* from the Hindu god of destruction. Bandar Pradesh. Shiva.

28.

A blazing nail of pain drove through Julia's head and she opened her eyes gingerly, anticipating a world of bright light that would only intensify the agony.

There was no light. Eyes open or shut, she could hardly tell the difference.

What just happened?

She was lying flat on the floor but the floor itself felt like it was sloping away. She thought that at any moment she might roll uncontrollably downhill. She remained motionless, careful not to let that happen.

A light, tiny but seemingly as brilliant as an arc welder, flared in the total darkness. She shielded her eyes with a hand, and saw a woman holding a small LED keychain light. After a moment, she recognized the woman—the American tourist that had accompanied the girl…*Sara*, that was her name. Now she remembered the girl… Carutius had known them somehow. And then…

"What in the hell just happened?" Sara demanded.

Julia looked at her again, aware now that her appearance had changed dramatically. Her face was caked with dust and sweat, and a trickle of blood ran from one eyebrow and down her cheek like a tear.

When she observed how different the woman looked, it was if the scales fell from Julia eyes. *Not just her*, she thought. *Everything is different.*

Indeed, as she looked around, she couldn't see anything that looked even vaguely familiar. Part of that might have been attributable to the inadequate illumination provided by the LED flashlight, but even that was an important detail. No lights. Were they even still in the museum? Her surroundings looked more like mineshaft after a cave in. Dust swirled in the air, coiling away as if caught by a draft, but she felt no breeze. Still, amidst the chaos, she began to discern familiar features of her environment. They were still in the Louvre; in fact, although nearly every trace of the exhibit was gone, she saw that they were still in La Chappelle gallery.

The wall coverings were gone, the old stone underneath riddled with fractures and in some places, gaping holes. The most dramatic difference however was the floor. An enormous crater had appeared in the center of the room, its focal point almost exactly where the display case had been. She had no memory of moving away from the area—perhaps Carutius had carried her, carried all of them—but the place where they had been standing was now a void, falling away into darkness. The dust motes, illuminated by the flashlight beam, were spiraling into the hole like water running down a drain.

She struggled to sit up. The disorientation she had felt upon waking persisted. Despite what her eyes told her, she had the feeling that if she moved the wrong way, she might pitch forward into the pit. The sensation reminded her of a carnival funhouse, but this was no mere trick of architecture or perspective.

She found the girl, huddled near Sara, and then she saw Carutius. The big man, who always seemed so confident and in control, now looked positively defeated. *He knows…*

"What did you do?" The accusation was out of her mouth before she knew it. "You caused this. Or you knew it was going to happen."

Carutius raised his head and met her stare. "I was trying to prevent it."

"Prevent what?" Sara demanded. "What is going on?"

The big man took a breath and let it out with a sigh. "It's not safe here. We should get outside."

"Screw that," Sara retorted. "We're all dead already. Lethal concentration of gamma rays…that's what you said. So the least you can do is answer my question."

Julia realized that her fingers were curled around a thin piece of plastic. It was the film badge dosimeter. She held it up and inspected it in the diffuse light, certain that she would discover that it had returned to normal…that she had only imagined the color change.

The center of the disk was dark.

Gamma ray exposure…followed by some kind of explosion… She knew of only one explanation for that: an atomic bomb.

Carutius considered Sara's demand for a moment. Then his gaze moved to Fiona and gradually the despair in his eyes was replaced by a measure of resolve. "Very well. I will answer your questions. But we must move away from here. It may be that we can do something…" His voice trailed off, unwilling or unable to elaborate. "Stay low. Crawl on the floor. The effect will be less pronounced as we move further away from the event horizon."

Event horizon? Had she heard that right? A point of no return, from which not even light could escape, and where time would appear to stand still.

Julia was an anthropologist, a student of history, not a

physicist, but she knew what an event horizons were, and she knew that they could be found only on the edge of a specific gravitational anomaly.

A black hole.

29.

King angled the Zodiac toward the riverboat's gangplank and killed the outboard, letting the craft's momentum take it the rest of the way. The brightly lit exterior deck of the floating casino was crowded with passengers gazing out in shocked amazement at the darkened city skyline, but it was a sure bet that at least some of them had noticed the approaching inflatable, and it was only a matter of time before Brown's security men were alerted to his return.

He slapped Brown's face a few times to rouse him, and hauled him into a sitting position, the barrel of the Uzi pressed against the base of the gambler's neck.

"Keep your mouth shut and you just might live through this," King growled. He didn't like the idea of walking in the front door using Brown as a human shield. There were too many variables in the situation, too many ways it could end badly. During the trip back to the riverboat, he'd racked his brain to come up with a better alternative, but there simply weren't any other options.

Brown offered no resistance as King guided him onto the gangplank. An armed man in formal wear, easily identifiable by his burly physique as one of the Alpha Dog mercenaries, stood at the top of the ramp. King stayed behind Brown, but made sure that the Uzi was visible.

"You know how this works," King called out. "Anyone makes a move against me and your boss is dead."

The man raised his hands in a placating gesture, his pistol pointing skyward, and offered a strange smile. "You'll get no trouble from us."

King did not relax his guard as he manhandled Brown up the gangplank and onto the reception deck. "Take me to Pradesh."

The security man slowly holstered his pistol and gestured for King to follow. The murmuring crowd parted to allow them through and a few moments later, they entered the deserted casino. "What's going on out there?" the guard asked. "An earthquake or something?"

King wondered if the inquiry was an attempt to distract him as a precursor to some treacherous action, but the man's tone sounded genuine. Brown probably hadn't shared the details of his plan with his hired guns. "That's what I'm here to find out. Your boss here knows, but he's not telling. That's why I need to talk to Pradesh."

"He's not my boss," the mercenary replied. "At least I don't think he is. We get all our orders by text message, and right now no one's answering."

"Don't expect that to change. Brainstorm is finished." King appraised the man a moment longer. "But if you're not ready for the unemployment line, I could probably find some work for you."

The mercenary gave him a sidelong glance. "You work for the government, right? A white hat?"

"Something like that."

The man chuckled. "Hell, why not? The name's Rick Chesler. I'd shake on it, but I can see you've got your hands full right now."

King nodded. He still had reservations about Chesler's abrupt change of loyalties, but he *was* a mercenary—changing loyalties to whoever cut the checks was part of the job. Plus, King's instincts told him the man was genuine—not all mercs were cold-blooded—and right now he needed all the help he could get.

The awakening was not merely an end to the long period of dormancy—something which itself possessed no meaning for the entity. It had not "known" that it had been sleeping any more than it was aware that it had existed at all prior to this moment in time. But now it knew.

It was not alive, not by any human definition at least. But like a virus, following the inexorable dictates of its internal chemistry, the entity was attuned to its surroundings and possessed of a singular purpose.

As with everything else in the universe, it was bound by the laws of nature. Existence required energy, and while the entity did not hunger for sustenance, the infusion of raw matter triggered a positive feedback loop; as mass was added, its internal gravity increased, which in turn attracted still more material, exponentially increasing intensity.

But that was not the purpose that now defined the entity.

It did not yet perceive the physical world, but it was self-aware, and it further grasped that this awareness was fractured, divided into several different parts. Though this essential awareness derived from the fractured parts of what it would eventually recognize as its mind, it understood that to take that next step, it would be necessary to bring together those parts, joining them to each other, and joining together with them.

To do that, it needed a proxy, and so cleaving off a hint of its own substance, it fashioned the manifestation, and sent it forth into the world.

30.

The journey from the ruins of the exhibition hall to the front exit of the Louvre was a blur to Fiona. She moved in a daze, struggling to make sense of everything that had happened.

First, there was Alexander's dire prognosis: *Gamma radiation... A lethal concentration...*

What did that even mean? She didn't feel any different. Maybe he'd been wrong. Or maybe the gamma rays would affect them differently. Maybe they'd all get mutant superpowers...like Bruce Banner in the *Incredible Hulk* comics.

Then the world had turned upside down.

Sara's flashlight, augmented by the occasional glow of battery operated emergency lights scattered throughout the corridors, revealed rubble strewn corridors that bore little resemblance to the ornate museum through which she had passed only a few minutes before.

Along the way, they encountered other museum patrons being guided to safety by Louvre personnel. The need for an alternate evacuation route became apparent when she stepped out into the Cour Napoleon—Napoleon's Courtyard—and caught a glimpse of the twisted steel frame that had once been the elaborate glass pyramid guarding the front entrance to the Louvre. The seventy-foot high structure groaned and creaked in the grip of tidal forces, the sound punctuated every few seconds by the noise of another glass pane breaking free and shattering on the ground below.

Fiona expected to find a cordon of emergency vehicles lined up outside, and beyond that, a world unaffected by the chaos that had swept out of the exhibition hall, but to her dismay she discovered that the legendary City of Lights was almost completely dark.

Alexander separated them from the crowd, but did not take them far. He directed them to sit on the ground, well away from any hazards, and without preamble, launched into a story. Although Sara had been the most vocal in demanding answers, Alexander's gaze remained fixed on Fiona as he spoke, a fact that did not escape the girl's notice.

"Nearly seventeen hundred years ago, the residents of the Bamiyan Valley, in what is now Afghanistan, encountered a strange phenomenon. They called it *Angra Mainyu*, believing it to be the devil of Zorastrian mythology. In reality, it was something even stranger: a micro black hole.

Julia shook her head in confusion. "I thought black holes were the remains of collapsed stars."

"The term 'black hole' applies to any region of space where the local gravity is so powerful that not even light can escape. It has long been believed that when a star uses up all of its fuel, its own gravity causes it to become a black hole—a concentration of stellar mass in something perhaps only a few miles in diameter. But that is only one type of black hole. Almost forty years ago, scientists posited the existence of very small black holes, caused spontaneously by cosmic rays or particle collisions. They have even tried to produce micro black holes at the Large Hadron Collider in Switzerland."

"They're making black holes in a laboratory?" Fiona said.

"That doesn't sound very smart."

"Most micro black holes are unstable and cease to exist in a matter of nanoseconds. Unlike stellar mass black holes, they don't have enough mass or energy to do any harm, much less achieve any kind of stability. The anomaly encountered by the Bamiyan villagers was different though. It was stable. Though probably only a few molecules in diameter, it had a mass equivalent to Mount Everest. The gravitational effects were localized; the event horizon was probably only about a meter, but anything—even particles of atmosphere—caught in the event horizon would have been added to its mass, increasing if only incrementally, the gravitational attraction. In time, it would have grown large enough to consume the entire planet."

"Hang on," Sara said. "You said this micro black hole was stable. What made it different?"

"And what stopped it?" Fiona added.

"I can no more tell you the reason for its stability than I can explain where it originated. But to answer your question Fiona..." Alexander cast a glance at Julia, and then chose his words carefully. "According to one report, the evil of Angra Mainyu ended when a traveling group of Buddhist monks taught the villagers a mantra."

"A mantra?" Julia made no effort to hide her skepticism.

Fiona however understood. Alexander had been there; one thousand seven hundred-odd years ago, the immortal Hercules had witness these events, had actively participated in them. Fiona also understood all too well the power that could have been unleashed with something seemingly as commonplace as a chanted mantra.

"A black hole is not simply super-condensed matter. If that were true, there would be little to fear from them. A black hole with the mass of a star would have the same gravity as the star itself—zero net change in the regional gravity equation. But at their core, black holes, and particularly micro black holes, consist of something called 'strange matter.' Strange matter appears to contravene the laws of physics governing the conservation of energy and matter. When strange matter interacts with normal matter—which is exactly what happens beyond the event horizon of a micro black hole—a change in mass occurs without the corresponding change in energy described by Einstein's famous equation."

Alexander must have sensed Fiona's confusion because he immediately left off the technical explanation. "When a black hole adds a ton of matter, its mass might increase by a thousand tons...or by nothing at all...depending on the specific frequency of the strange matter at that exact moment.

"My hypothesis is that the monks' chant found the specific acoustic frequency that cancelled out, and possibly even reversed, the strange matter reaction."

Realization dawned and the words were out before Fiona could stop herself. "They sang it to sleep."

A faint smile crossed Alexander's rough visage and he nodded. "That's exactly what they did."

"You're serious about this," Julia said. She glanced at Sara and then at Fiona. "And you believe him?"

"I believe what happened in there," Sara shot back. "So unless you've got a better answer..."

"What did happen?" Fiona asked.

"The black hole was dormant, but it had not destabilized. Instead, it simply lay there on the ground, smaller than even a mote of dust. The people of the region converted to Buddhism, and consecrated the ground where the struggle with the black hole had occurred. Hundreds of years later, they fashioned two enormous statues of the Buddha, the bodies carved from the sandstone cliffs and the features molded of a stucco. The black hole itself was incorporated into the stucco, perhaps intentionally, as a way to prevent it from accidentally being reawakened."

Julia sat up straight, realization finally dawning. "Until the

Taliban came along and blew them up."

Alexander nodded. "It's a wonder that the explosions didn't reactivate the black hole."

"So what caused it to happen tonight?" Even as Fiona asked it, the last piece of the puzzle fell into place. "You knew it was going to happen. That's why you were here. That sound you were playing...that was a recording of monks chanting, wasn't it?"

Alexander nodded guiltily. "I arranged for the pieces of the Buddhas to be brought out of Afghanistan in hopes that I could identify and isolate the black hole. I thought that I had taken sufficient precautions—the recorded mantra, as you have so astutely deduced—but it seems I miscalculated."

Then a conspiratorial smile settled on his lips. "However, there may be—"

A sudden cry from the courtyard interrupted him. His head swiveled to locate the source, and Fiona looked as well.

A stampede was in progress. A group of museum patrons who had been huddled in a corner of the courtyard formed by the meeting of the Denon and Sully wings, was now moving as a panicked mass toward them. Behind them, Fiona saw what had prompted the terrified exodus.

An enormous dark spot, easily ten feet high, had appeared on the exterior wall of the palace. Fiona knew that it was no mere shadow because there was no light source outside to create such a powerful contrast; indeed, the dark spot was only visible because, unlike the rest of the museum, it reflected not even a hint of moonlight. It was absolutely black, the complete absence of light. It was exactly what she imagined the black hole must look like.

And it was moving.

Fiona watched in stunned silence as the dark spot detached from the wall and began moving into the courtyard. She saw that it was not simply an amorphous void; there was the suggestion of a central shape, surrounded by radiating tendrils of darkness, which writhed like snakes in every direction. Her first thought was that it resembled an octopus or jellyfish. The tentacles wiggled out ahead of it, seeming to grasp the ground and pull it forward into the courtyard. As it advanced, Fiona saw that the part of the museum wall from which it had issued was gone. It hadn't broken apart, but simply erased from existence as if it had evaporated into smoke.

Alexander jumped to his feet and scooped Fiona up with one massive arm. "Run!"

His shout galvanized Sara and Julia into action, and they followed as he darted out of the path of the onrushing crowd.

The black shape continued forward, no faster than a jogging pace but relentless as a heat-seeking missile. Beyond the edge of the perimeter of the courtyard, the crowd began to disperse in all directions but the dark thing did not alter course to pursue any of them.

Alexander halted as soon as they were clear of the mob, and he turned to observe the shape's journey. From his embrace, Fiona saw that several other evacuees had stopped as well, their curiosity evidently overcoming the instinct to flee. A few, like bystanders viewing the aftermath of a traffic accident, actually began moving closer to the thing.

"Stay back!" Alexander warned.

His command went unheeded. One of the group, a boy perhaps only a couple years older than Fiona, with long stringy blond hair and numerous facial piercings, wearing low hanging plaid shorts and a Tony Hawk T-shirt, fell in behind the shape. He moved slowly, poised to run at the first sign of trouble, but when it became evident that the shape was oblivious to his presence, he quickened his step, matching its pace and peering into the lightless mass for some clue about its nature.

A murmur of voices issued from the crowd, some echoing

Alexander's plea for caution, others—mostly from the teenager's peer group—daring him to get closer. The boy raised a hand, testing the air, and sensing no peril, stepped around the moving shape and placed himself in its path.

Fiona gasped as the shape engulfed the curious boy. For just a moment it paused as if the encounter had forced it to make a decision, but the tendrils resumed reaching out, pulling the shadowy mass forward. As it moved, the boy was revealed, standing motionless exactly as he had a few seconds before. Fiona waited for his reaction, hoping to see him give some indication that the black mass was harmless, half-expecting him to crumple lifelessly to the ground...but he did not move. He did not even seem to breathe.

The dark shape cleared the courtyard and then abruptly shifted left, angling toward the open space separating the end of the Denon wing from the Jardin des Tuileries, and to all appearances, completely ignoring the shocked spectators.

Fiona felt Alexander's hold on her loosen, and after setting her down, he moved slowly toward where the impulsive teenager still stood statue still. Her own curiosity aroused, Fiona caught up to Alexander, her gaze now riveted on the motionless figure. She knew that her desire to discover the youth's fate was little different from the urge that had prompted the young man to approach the nightmarish entity, but she had to know.

Other museum patrons were closing on the spot, compelled by the same craving for answers and she heard one of them gasp. "My God. He's been turned to stone."

Fiona saw it too. The boy had been transformed utterly. His appearance was unchanged; the color and texture of his skin, hair and clothes were as distinct and individual as they had been in life. But where once there had been a living organism of flesh and blood and bone, wrapped in clothes woven of cotton and synthetic fibers, there was now only a lifeless mannequin made of what looked like polished stone.

Fiona shuddered and shrank into Alexander's embrace. "That's...horrible," she said, choking back a sob. "A black hole can do that?"

For some reason, Alexander's answer and the tone in which it was delivered was even more shocking to her than the curious youth's fate. In a voice that verged on pure trepidation, the immortal Hercules answered simply: "I don't know."

31.

King did not bother with the doorknob, much less signal his presence with a knock. Instead, he delivered a decisive kick that slammed the flimsy door aside. Then he propelled Brown through the opening, into the control room, following close behind with the Uzi leveled. Chesler remained in the hallway, guarding the approach, though his vigilance was probably unnecessary. None of the Alpha Dog mercenaries had given the slightest indication that their employer's fate mattered one bit; if Chesler's defection was any indication, they all seemed to sense that working for Brainstorm was a dead end.

Pradesh started at the intrusion, jolting upright in his chair, but otherwise made no move as King aimed the gun at him. The Indian hacker's initial surprise quickly passed, his expression giving way to something that looked like satisfaction. "I didn't expect to see you again," he said with a chuckle.

King ignored the attempt at banter. "Brainstorm's finished," he declared. "Shut it down."

Pradesh glanced at Brown, who had recovered from King's shove and was now leaning against a bulkhead, glowering but saying nothing. Pradesh then looked back at King, smiling in a mockery of innocence. "Shut what down?" He gestured to the bank of monitor screens, all of which were dark. "There's been some kind of blackout. I'm not connected to anything at the moment."

"You know goddamn well what I'm talking about. The quantum computers. You built them, you control them. Now turn them off."

Pradesh folded his arms over his chest and leaned back in his chair. "Why on Earth would I want to do that?"

King stabbed the Uzi's barrel at him menacingly. "A lot of reasons come to mind. Saving your lousy ass is probably first on the list."

Pradesh seemed unfazed, amused even. "You really have no idea what's going on."

The hacker's demeanor bothered King. This wasn't false bravado or posturing; Pradesh did not appear to be the least bit troubled by the threat of violence. King chose his next move carefully. "I know that Brown—or rather Brown pretending to be Brainstorm—hired you to attack the global power network." He glanced at the gambler, who remained defiant, giving no hint as to whether King's supposition was on the mark. "You built that quantum computer to control a virus that could break down any security firewalls and adapt to any defensive measures. Impressive stuff. I'm sure you're worth every penny he paid you, but I don't think that check is going to clear."

"Money." Pradesh scoffed. He glanced at Brown again, making no effort to hide his contempt. "Everybody in this world thinks that you can buy anything. That if you dangle enough money in front of someone, they'll be your faithful dog.

"You are correct in one respect. That's exactly what Mr. Brown, or rather his somewhat comical alter-ego Brainstorm, hired me to do." He then leaned forward conspiratorially. "But that's not what I did."

King saw a look of surprise flash across Brown's countenance, and barely managed to hide a similar reaction. He had misjudged Pradesh. Fortunately, the hacker appeared eager to boast about his accomplishments. King lowered the Uzi a notch and tried a different tack. "I thought that business about a quantum computer sounded like a lot of sci-fi horseshit. You conned, him right?"

Pradesh's visage went dark with barely restrained rage. "I did no such thing," he said, enunciating each word to underscore his ire.

King feigned a skeptical shrug to hide his satisfaction at how quickly Pradesh had taken the bait.

"The quantum computer is a masterpiece, and more valuable than Brainstorm—" The hacker again made no effort to disguise his contempt, "—could possibly have realized. I could have done what he wanted in my sleep, but he was too ignorant to realize that. Instead, he gave me what I wanted; the money and resources to build the quantum computer. He never even suspected."

"You're lying," Brown said, his own anger rising. "The hardware was assembled at Jovian Technologies."

"Based on my specifications."

"I had your work checked independently. Every design, every line of code was reviewed. You did exactly what I hired you to do."

Pradesh dismissed him with a wave. "Your so-called experts had no idea what I was doing. They saw only what I allowed them to see."

King suddenly understood that, whatever Brown's scheme had been—and he was now convinced that his earlier supposition about Brown's plan to sabotage the power grid was correct—it had nothing at all to do with the phenomena he had earlier witnessed. The real threat was evidently something much worse.

"Talk is cheap," he interjected, maintaining his façade of disinterest. "What did you do, write a program to steal credit card numbers or something?"

Pradesh's seemed to choke on his rage, but then with an effort, mastered himself. "I'll tell you what I did," he said in a low voice. "You know who I am, right? What they call me?"

King cocked his head sideways. "Shiva, right?"

"Do you recall what Robert Oppenheimer said after the first atomic bomb test? 'I am become Death, the destroyer of worlds.' He was quoting from Hindu scripture, the Bhagavad Gita, in reference to the Hindu deity—Shiva, the destroyer." Pradesh snorted derisively. "Oppenheimer was arrogant. What did he do? Create a weapon that could destroy a city?"

King blinked at him. In drawing Pradesh out, he had unleashed the hacker's inner madman. "But you can do better, right?"

"I have done better. I have let loose the true destroyer of worlds."

"Do tell?"

"A primordial black hole," Pradesh said, almost reverently. "Dormant for centuries, hidden in a statue of the Buddha. I discovered how to awaken it."

King's mind was racing to process what the Indian was saying. As much as he wanted to disbelieve, he knew better. The earthquake had followed Brown's activation of the quantum phone by only a few minutes. That could not be a coincidence. As crazy as it sounded, Pradesh's claim just might be true, yet he couldn't let the hacker know that he believed every word. He turned to Brown and none-too-discreetly wiggled a finger beside his temple and mouthed the word: "Cuckoo."

"That's why I needed a quantum computer," Pradesh continued. "Something that functions on the same principles as the black hole itself. And it worked. The QC isolated the frequency that would activate the dormant black hole. But that's only part of it. You see, the QC and the black hole are now linked together—mind and body, as it were. I didn't just wake the destroyer up, I gave it a brain."

"You did all this yourself? Found a...what did you call it? A primordial black hole just laying around, and figured out how to turn it on? You're a hacker." He filled the word with disgust, as if describing something he might scrape off the sole of his shoe. "What do you know about black holes?"

"I had some help. There are others who share my vision."

"And what exactly is your vision? What is it that you want? You said you don't care about money? So what then?"

"You really haven't heard a thing I've said. I want to destroy. Everything."

King's amazement at the boast momentarily overcame his ability to play act the skeptic. "For God's sake, why?"

"Because I can." Pradesh's simple reply revealed just how truly unhinged he had become. Then he continued in the same reverential tone. "Do you know what happens when you enter a black hole? You experience infinity. It is like looking into...no, it's like being one with the mind of God."

King pondered what to do next. Pradesh had made no effort to deceive him or withhold information and he knew that with just a little more prompting, the man would volunteer the names of other members his suicide/doomsday cult, but if the hacker's claims were true, that knowledge would be of little benefit. He was running out of time. "Fine," he declared, lowering the Uzi and taking out one of the improvised claymores he'd scavenged from the dead Russian commando. "I'll just blow up your quantum computer."

Pradesh offered a coy smile. "The computer isn't here. It doesn't have a fixed location. That's the beauty of it."

King immediately grasped the significance of the answer and recalled what he had overheard in Brown's office. *The phones*! He switched the IED to his left hand and dug out the quantum device. "And what happens if I smash this?"

A faint glimmer of anxiety rippled through Pradesh's mask of confidence, and King pressed the point. "No, that wouldn't be enough would it? I'd have to take out all of them, all ten."

Pradesh's increasing discomfort verified King's supposition. He started for the door, but at that instant, a scream—not one, but dozens of terrified cries—echoed through the corridor. Chesler ducked his head into the room, his eyes wide with apprehension. "Hey, man. I think something bad is happening up there."

Amid the sudden tumult, King heard laughter.

"Too late," Pradesh chortled. "It's already here."

32.

Suvorov slipped over the railing and dropped into a ready stance on the riverboat's forward deck. Two more Spetsnaz commandos—all that remained of his original team—clambered over right behind him, their weapons at the ready. The boat was now eerily quiet; although the spacious deck at the aft end was crowded with passengers, the noise of the party that had masked the team's previous entry was gone. Still, no one seemed to notice their arrival.

He had followed King's journey back to the riverboat from a distance. At first, this was due to his inability to take any action, stranded as he was in a boat with a shattered outboard. He had managed to contact the members of the team in the lead boat—thank goodness they had bought waterproof two-way radios—and arranged for them to come and get him. One of the men from the trailing boat had also radioed for help, his need slightly more urgent since he had a broken arm and treading water with only one good hand was rapidly wearing him out. That man's teammate had not made contact, and Suvorov feared the worst.

Two men dead—Ian, dead—and another man badly injured.

And we don't even have the man we came for.

Later, when he had rendezvoused with the surviving members of the team—the injured man had been left in the damaged boat—he held back because he was curious about his opponent's movements. Brown's rescuer had inexplicably turned back to the riverboat. That abrupt change of course had occurred right after the earthquake that had not only plunged the city into darkness, but also blanketed all the radio frequencies with impenetrable static. Suvorov didn't know how the events were connected, but at least now his prey was in a fixed location and was evidently not going anywhere.

Suvorov signaled for his men to advance. He knew that this time, things were going to get ugly. With only the three of them, the mere threat of violence would not suffice to control the situation. They would have to take decisive action. They had removed the sound suppressors from the Uzis; there would be shooting, and this time, noise and chaos—not stealth—would be their greatest ally. Suvorov had made it clear that they weren't to waste any ammunition on warning shots.

But before the team could make their presence known, all hell broke loose on the party deck. Suvorov halted the team as the silence was broken by a chorus of frantic screams, followed by noise of a rushing mob. An instant later, the deck leading along the side of the superstructure was filled with dozens of passengers, men in tuxedos and women in evening gowns, all running headlong from whatever had triggered the stampede. Suvorov's team was completely exposed but none of the passengers seemed to give them even a second glance as they pushed past, seeking the forward section of the riverboat. Off to the side, splashes in the river's surface indicated that some at the rear of the pack had chosen to simply jump overboard. Behind the frantic crowd, about fifty feet from where the Spetsnaz team stood frozen in place, the source of the panic came into view.

The thing defied description. It seemed at once both

insubstantial, like a cloud of black smoke, and as solid as granite. Towering above the fleeing horde, at least ten feet high, its mass filled the narrow gap between the bulkheads of the superstructure and the deck railing. Long black tendrils squirmed out ahead of it, grasping the deck to draw it forward, yet the whole thing moved as smoothly as a bead of quicksilver.

What happened next left Suvorov almost paralyzed with disbelief. One of the tentacles abruptly shot forward, stretching out like a frog's tongue snatching a fly out the air, and speared into the fleeing crowd. Several of the passengers—everyone in the path of the snaking protrusion—simply evaporated, vanishing from existence. Nothing remained; no shreds of clothing, no blood, not even ashes. It was as if every molecule of each person touched by the tentacle, had come apart in an instant.

But not all of them.

One man, who had almost reached the Spetsnaz team's position, was caught by the tendril and instantly snatched back—alive and evidently unharmed—into the main body of the thing.

Then it happened a second time.

"Down!" Suvorov shouted, throwing himself flat.

A tentacle shot past, missing him by scant inches though he neither heard nor felt any disturbance. Two men and a woman, all of whom had already pushed past the commandos, vanished in a puff, and then the snake-thing reached through the space those victims had occupied, gripped another man who was climbing the railing in preparation to leap overboard, and yanked him back. Suvorov felt something brush his back, the unlucky man's thrashing feet, and then he was gone, enveloped completely by the dark mass.

The thing continued to move forward. Thirty feet away... Twenty... It towered above them like a tornado. The advancing tendrils that drew it onward, each one as thick as a tree trunk, were only inches away.

A crescendo of gunfire erupted beside Suvorov. One of his men was firing his Uzi into the thing.

There was no sign of damage. The bullets vanished into it without any visible effect, but remarkably, the shape halted.

The gun fell silent as the magazine ran out.

And the monster moved again.

33.

Julia closed her eyes. *This has to be a nightmare*, she thought. *When I open my eyes, I'll be in my bed, and there will be an empty Häagen Dazs carton on the nightstand.*

She knew better. Even in her wildest dreams, she never could have imagined miniature black holes coming to life, destroying the Louvre and turning people to stone. And when she opened her eyes again, nothing had changed.

Carutius was examining the petrified boy while Fiona and Sara stood a few steps away, hugging each other. The black shape was long gone, sliding noiselessly around the corner of the museum and headed to God only knew where.

"That thing…" Fiona shuddered. "It's like a basilisk."

Carutius glanced back quizzically, prompting her to add, "It's from Harry Potter. A snake that can turn people into stone just by looking at them."

"I'm familiar with the mythological creature," he rumbled, with what almost sounded like approval. "In this case, our basilisk triggered a strange matter reaction. It changed the atomic mass of every particle in his body, and he was literally turned to stone. Mostly silicon if I'm not mistaken."

"Why?" Julia asked. "I mean, this doesn't make any sense. Black holes are just supposed to suck everything in. They're not supposed to wander around turning people to stone."

"Black holes don't 'suck,'" Carutius said. "They exert a gravitational influence that attracts matter and causes it to fall into the event horizon. But you are correct. Something else is going on here. Everything that we know, or rather think we know, about black holes is based on theories. It may be that there is some kind of consciousness at work here."

"That thing is alive?" Julia said.

"Not in a conventional sense, but yes, it is conceivable." He put a hand on Fiona's shoulder. "And it might be that you can communicate with it."

"Me?" Fiona squeaked, but then a look of understanding came over her. "You mean using the mother tongue."

Julia gaped at them but withheld comment. Carutius and the girl both seemed to know a lot about what was going on, and that scared the hell out of her. *Who are these people?*

Fiona's brow creased and she shook her head. "But I don't know the mother tongue. I barely knew enough to stop the golem."

"You know more than you realize. Remember what you told me before? How the artwork in the museum and the fragments of the Buddha statues spoke you? The knowledge is within you, and I believe that together, we can unlock that knowledge and use it to control this thing."

"Control it," Fiona murmured. "I could sing it to sleep again, like the monks did."

Carutius seemed to frown but then nodded. "Yes. It will be difficult. You will have to trust me implicitly, and do exactly as I instruct."

Sara shook her head. "I'll be damned if I'm going to stand by and let you take her chasing after that thing."

"Dr. Fogg, the fate of this world is in the balance, and

Fiona might be the only person who can tip the balance in our favor."

"We don't even know where it is."

As if to punctuate Sara's reply, a loud crump echoed from the museum and reverberated through the ground beneath their feet. Carutius gazed back at the ruined building and raised a hand to silence further comment. He listened for a moment then turned back to them and said: "I don't think we'll have to go anywhere."

The entity's awareness of itself and the world in which it existed increased exponentially as the disparate fragments of its consciousness were assimilated. It had begun this process knowing nothing more than the impulsive need—an attraction as basic as magnetism or nuclear force—to bring those pieces together.

The manifestation had been drawn inexorably to those pieces, sensing that they were together in one physical location, even though the concept of location had no meaning to the entity, at least, not at the beginning. Obstacles lay in its path, an utterly alien environment of which it was not even truly aware, but like a bead of water following the path of least resistance, it moved around these, or when that did not suffice, changed them. The latter was no mean feat; there was a price to be paid for altering the substance of reality.

It comprehended all of this now. As the fragments of the consciousness—the mind—were gathered by the manifestation, its awareness of the environment and its grasp of causal relationships blossomed into existence. No longer was it driven purely by physical forces; no, now it guided the manifestation purposefully. The pieces of the mind lay scattered before it, moving to and fro in an effort to avoid assimilation, but the entity guided the manifestation intently, focusing on collecting each one in turn. The entity sensed another piece of the mind added, and its awareness leaped forward again. It was nearly complete. Only three more remained.

Now something different. The manifestation was encountering resistance—a storm of matter that it could not avoid. A threat! Surely nothing that could endanger the manifestation, but the relentless barrage of dense particles had halted its advance, forced it to change each of the incoming projectiles. Neutrons were stripped away in an instant, metals changed to insubstantial gaseous elements, but the entity felt its power waning.

This threat had to be neutralized.

To do that, it needed to feed.

34.

King grasped Brown by the collar and hauled him erect. The gambler might not have had any clue about Pradesh's actual agenda, much less any ability to alter its outcome, and dragging him around was probably going to end up being more trouble than it was worth, but he'd gone through too much to take the bastard down. He wasn't about to simply turn the man loose. A single bullet probably would have resolved the dilemma, but that wasn't King's style.

"Chesler! Grab him." King pointed to Pradesh. As the Alpha Dog mercenary moved into the room, King thrust his captive into the corridor. He kept one hand on Brown's collar and the other on the grip of the Uzi pressed against the base of the gambler's spine, pre-empting any displays of resistance on the latter's part. As he made his way back toward the casino, the noise of the disturbance outside grew more intense, though not quite loud enough to drown out Pradesh's insane cackle.

A black hole, he thought. *A black hole with a brain, no less. God damn it. Why can't the crazies just stick to weaponized Ebola and suitcase nukes?*

Five years ago, he probably would have dismissed Pradesh's

claim out of hand, but he'd seen a lot of impossible things since then—mythological monsters, Neanderthals, golem. He'd survived them all. Hell, he'd found a way to stop them all.

The screams had dwindled by the time he reached the casino, and when he threw open the door to the aft deck, he found it empty. Or rather, almost empty. Three human forms were visible, standing at the railing and seemingly gazing out at the dark water. But they didn't move. The three appeared frozen in place, as still as statues. King resisted the urge to make a closer inspection; he wasn't sure he wanted to know what had happened to them.

The distinctive crack of an unsilenced Uzi grabbed his attention and he instinctively drew back against the superstructure, looking for cover. The shots had originated along the port side of the riverboat. As far as he knew—and he had taken a crash course in physics as part of Deep Blue's new intensive educational program for Chess Team—black holes didn't use semi-automatic weapons. Something else was going on. He dragged Brown behind him toward the corner and peeked around it.

His first impression was that someone had blocked access to the deck with a black velvet curtain. Ten feet high, with shadowy protrusions spread out behind it, the thing didn't look like any kind of black hole he'd ever read about.

Pradesh must have gotten bad information. It was impossible to see a black hole because their gravity was so strong that no light could reflect back to reach the human eye. Nor did this apparition appear to be causing any gravitational or relativistic disturbances. This thing, as weird as it was, could not be a black hole.

And if it's not a black hole, maybe bullets can hurt it. He hefted his own Uzi and started to take aim, but something brushed past him before he could pull the trigger.

Pradesh.

The hacker had broken free from Chesler's grip and dashed past King toward the dark shape. He spread his arms wide as he ran toward it, shouting: "I'm ready!"

As soon as he touched the thing, Pradesh stopped moving. King didn't notice any other distinctive physical changes, but something was different. The hacker's sudden silence and lack of movement was profoundly unnatural.

"Guess that 'mind of God' stuff didn't work out for you," King muttered. "So much for infinity and beyond."

Suddenly, Pradesh disappeared. It was as if he were nothing more than a human shaped balloon popped by a needle; one instant he was there, and then nothing. King was still trying to digest this when he realized something had changed. The dark shape was moving. Toward him.

Tentacles snaked out along the deck, pulling the thing along with a smoothness that concealed just how fast it was moving. King barely had time to pull back from the corner before the writhing tendrils reached that spot.

He spun and aimed for the gangplank and the waiting Zodiac, heaving Brown ahead of him. A glance over his shoulder showed the thing creeping relentlessly onward, following him—or so it appeared—like a bloodhound. Then he saw Chesler, riveted in place and staring at the dark mass—not literally turned to stone, but petrified nonetheless. King almost called out to the Alpha Dog contractor, but he knew it was already too late.

He pitched Brown into the Zodiac and followed, shoving the rubber boat away from its mooring as he heaved himself over the inflatable gunwale. The black shape slid past Chesler, missing him by mere inches, and oozed onto the gangplank, just as King fired up the outboard.

The water around the riverboat was crowded with passengers who had sought escape from the dark shape by leaping overboard. Many of them were struggling to stay afloat, the cold water and their sodden clothes conspiring to sap their strength. Several heads turned in King's direction in the instant that the outboard roared to life; frantic hands grasped the sides of the rubber boat. King felt a pang of guilt as he opened the throttle and pushed through their midst.

The shadow thing was right behind him, pulling itself across the surface of the Seine as if the water were no different from the solid deck of the riverboat. Its tentacle-like protrusions barely left a ripple as it reached out again and again to draw itself forward. The screws of the Zodiac's motor were gradually propelling the craft faster than the shape appeared capable of moving, but if King stopped to help even a single beleaguered swimmer, the thing would catch him. Moreover, he knew that he wouldn't be doing anyone a favor by performing a rescue; the creature, whatever it was, was coming after him, and King had a pretty good idea why.

The swimmers he'd already passed thrashed desperately to get out of the thing's path, and for the most part, none felt its deadly touch. A few unlucky souls however lost the race and vanished in an instant as the tendrils brushed them. Then King saw something that all but confirmed his hypothesis.

A tendril snaked out to the shape's left and plucked a man from the water. King only caught a glimpse of the man's horrified face as he was pulled back, still very much alive, into the dark mass, but he nonetheless recognized the victim as one of the ten who had received a quantum phone from Brown earlier in the evening.

He recalled Pradesh's words. *I gave it a brain.* The hacker had been only half-right about that. His quantum computer had awakened the black hole, or whatever it was, and evidently imparted some rudimentary degree of awareness to it, but it didn't literally have its *brain*—the quantum computer network—and correcting that condition was its only priority. It was hunting down the quantum phone devices, collecting them together and integrating them physically into its being.

King knew less about quantum physics than he did about black holes, but he knew that one of the most difficult concepts for the novice physicist to grasp was the idea of quantum colocation. Experiments had proven that subatomic particles could literally be in two places at the same time. Pradesh's quantum computer seemed to take advantage of this property; the hacker had said the device didn't have a physical location, but what he had really meant was that it existed in ten different locations simultaneously; the ten quantum phones. The dark shape was evidently entangled with the quantum computer, linked to and benefiting from the artificial intelligence subroutine, but it needed more. It needed to be in physical contact with the computer. That was the sole reason it had come to the riverboat, where all ten recipients of the devices were clustered together like fish in a barrel. It wasn't too much of a stretch to believe that with each assimilation, its intelligence multiplied.

How many has it already taken? Am I the last?

The quantum phone in his pocket suddenly felt very heavy. He felt an almost overwhelming urge to hurl it away or crush it out of existence, but what would that accomplish? At best, he would throw it off his scent and damage a tenth of the thing's "brain" but there was no guarantee of even that. No, until he understood the threat better, hanging onto the device was imperative. Keeping the phone was probably his best chance at figuring out how to beat the dark shape, and as long as he kept it in his possession, he knew where the thing would go next. He'd just have to make sure he kept it at a safe distance.

Safe, he thought disparagingly. *This thing can walk on water. Nowhere is safe.*

With the outboard throttle wide open, the riverboat and its surrounding crowd of fleeing passengers receded into the distance. King lost sight of the dark mass, but his last glimpse of it had shown it moving only about half as fast as the Zodiac.

That at least was something in his favor.

A faint orange glow radiated up from the darkened cityscape—fires resulting from the earthquake, probably fed by ruptured gas lines—but it did little to illuminate the immediate area. King eased off the throttle, searching for some hint of the riverbank. He was uncertain about leaving the river. On solid ground, moving through streets that were probably choked with debris and filled with frightened survivors, his lead on the monster would quickly evaporate. But he couldn't stay in the Zodiac forever.

He needed to make contact with Deep Blue and Aleman. The latter's technical expertise would be invaluable in figuring out how the quantum computer worked and how to shut it down. He checked his Chess Team phone again; still no signal. The citywide power outage would have knocked out the local cell phone network, but his phone was satellite capable, designed to provide instant communication almost anywhere in the world. Solar flares and other electromagnetic phenomena could disrupt the signal. Was something like that at work here? Or had the quantum device somehow taken control of Chess Team's network?

Brown might be able to tell him, but King doubted the sullen gambler would willingly offer him any assistance.

A subtle change in the texture of the surrounding darkness alerted King to the nearness of the riverbank and he hastily reversed the screws just as the nose of the Zodiac crunched into a sloping concrete abutment, sliding several feet up its angled face before coming to rest. The sudden stop pitched King forward, but he quickly regained his equilibrium and cautiously extended a foot out into the darkness. He felt solid ground beneath the sole of his shoe.

He grasped Brown's biceps and hauled the gambler to his feet. "Let's go."

Though he was no match for King in terms of physical

strength, Brown tried to pull free. "I'm not going anywhere with you. And I don't think you're going to sucker punch me again and drag my ass all over Paris. Not with that thing chasing you."

King resisted the urge to cajole the gambler, instead saying: "What makes you think it's after me?"

"Isn't it obvious? It's after the quantum computer, which is synched to your phone." Brown's voice took on an air of triumph. "You could throw it away of course. Funny thing about the quantum computer, though. Do you know why I didn't just turn it on and set it loose? Why I had to go to the trouble of finding ten different carriers for the synchronization?"

King was grateful that the darkness hid his anxious expression. He wanted to hear Brown's explanation, but time was short and odds were good that the gambler was simply stalling. He feigned disinterest. "I'm sure you just did it because that kook Pradesh told you to. He was the expert on quantum mechanics, not you."

"Give me some credit, Sigler." Brown's voice was tight, and King knew the barb had stuck. "It was my plan from the beginning, and I learned everything I could about the subject before I gave Pradesh one red cent."

"You're a regular super-genius," King goaded. "You clearly had a grasp on scientific principles when you tried to engineer a virus that would turn everyone into mindless drones. And when you almost set the atmosphere on fire with Bluelight."

Brown ignored the taunt, which is exactly what King had hoped he would do. "The quantum devices aren't just synched to cell phones; they're synched with the person who uses that phone."

"You're the one activated it. Maybe that thing is chasing you, not me."

"It doesn't work like that. That was Pradesh's breakthrough. You see, when you use a computer, or even an Internet capable cell phone, a quantum connection is made. A computer, on a level we can barely comprehend, gets used to its user. The quantum computer exploits that connectivity. It *knows* you. So you see King, there's nothing you can do. It's going to catch you and it's going to kill you, and there's not a thing you can do to stop it." Brown allowed himself a satisfied pause before continuing. "I have no intention of going with you. I suppose you could knock me out again, but is it really worth it for you to drag me along? That thing is coming for you."

"Maybe I should just shoot you."

Brown gave an indifferent shrug. "Suit yourself. You've had plenty of chances to do that before, and yet here I am. Maybe you don't have the stones for cold blooded murder."

King didn't answer. He wasn't sure he believed in Brown's crazy theory about the quantum network being linked to him personally, but the gambler was right about everything else. He couldn't take Brown with him, and he knew he couldn't simply gun him down.

Before he could resolve the dilemma, a new voice reached out of the darkness from somewhere above. "King? Is that you?"

The familiar voice startled King, but he quickly recovered his wits and put a name to the speaker. "Chesler? How in the hell did you get up there?"

"I found a shortcut," the mercenary said with just a hint of mischief in his voice. A flashlight beam stabbed out of the darkness from the top of the concrete wall and searched him out. "That thing is following you. It will be here any second. You've got to get moving."

King turned to his captive. "I think I can drag your ass around a little while longer. Do I need to give you another concussion, or will you come along willingly?"

Brown glowered, but nodded and climbed out of the Zodiac. King kept his Uzi trained on Brown as they scrambled up the embankment to where Chesler stood with the flashlight, just beyond a low stone wall that separated the river bank from a paved roadway. As he clambered over the barrier, he repeated his earlier question to the security contractor. "Seriously. How did you get here ahead of us?"

Chesler waggled the flashlight. "I could see where I was going. Took a straight line and came ashore just a ways from here. And…I had some help."

Two more lights flashed on, transfixing King with their beams. King shaded his eyes from the sudden glare, and he could just make out a trio of men standing alongside Chesler, wearing dark clothes and holding guns identical to the one he now carried. He didn't recognize their faces, which were no longer concealed behind black balaclavas, but he knew immediately who they were.

King shook his head and gave a defeated sigh. "Chesler, you're fired."

35.

Suvorov stared at the two men illuminated by the flashlights of his Spetsnaz teammates. One of them was the objective of the mission that had brought him to Paris. The other had killed Kharitonov.

What could be simpler? Take one, kill the other. That's what he knew he should do. All of his military training could have been summed up in a single phrase: the mission comes first. No matter what else happened, accomplishing the mission should have been his first priority. Not fifteen minutes earlier, he would have carried out both tasks without hesitation...even with a sense of satisfaction.

But damn it, a lot had happened in the last fifteen minutes.

He didn't know exactly *what* had happened. When the city had been plunged into darkness, he hadn't really paid heed, but that thing he'd faced on the riverboat...*what in God's name was that?*

It had been only inches from him when something had caused it to reverse course. A few seconds later, he'd met the SVR undercover operative—the man now going by the name

Chesler—who, while providing a few answers, didn't really know anything of use. One thing he'd said however, still echoed in Suvorov's head.

It went after them.

He took a step forward, putting himself at arm's length from both men. The one Chesler had called 'King,' evidently an American operative, had been relieved of his weapons, but Suvorov knew from experience that the man was still very dangerous.

"What is that thing?" he asked.

King gazed back impassively. "Honestly, I have no idea."

"I don't think you're being truthful. I want to know what you know, even if it's merely a supposition." He glanced past King, toward the dark river. "We aren't going anywhere until I get some answers. How long do you think you have before it gets here?"

King gave an odd smile, and then to Suvorov's amazement, began talking. His account was succinct, like a military briefing. He talked about quantum phones and a crazed Indian who had believed he was unleashing a black hole upon the world.

"I don't think it is a black hole," King finished, "but it must be something like that. What it did to Pradesh..."

Suvorov nodded. He'd witnessed some of the fleeing passengers evaporating before his eyes and had found others evidently turned to stone. It seemed more like a demonic monster from a folktale. And didn't those stories usually end with the hero slaying the monster?

"Bullets slowed it down," Suvorov revealed. "There has to be a way to kill it."

King seemed genuinely surprised by this news. "I've got some ideas about that myself, but I'll need time. And a little breathing room. So, if you don't have any more questions, it might be a good idea for us to get moving."

"Where should we go?"

"Anywhere is better than here." Despite the urgency of his previous statement, King studied Suvorov a moment. "You're Russian special forces, aren't you? Spetsnaz? I think I know why you're here, and it's got nothing to do with stopping that thing."

Suvorov shrugged, confirming nothing King had said. "I think right now, the immediate problem takes precedence over other considerations."

"And later? If we survive this?"

Suvorov didn't answer. "You mentioned something before, something the Indian told you about where it came from."

"He said it was hidden in a Buddhist statue. I'm not really sure what he meant by that."

"I think I know," Suvorov said. "I might not know what it is, but I think I know exactly where it came from."

36.

Alexander led them back into the ruins of the Louvre. Fiona stayed close to him, and Sara stayed close to her, with Julia a few steps behind. As they picked their way through the rubble and entered the darkened museum that had once been a kingly palace, the curator gave a little gasp.

"I can't believe it. Hundreds of years' worth of history…all ruined."

Fiona couldn't quite fathom the woman's grief. In her life, she'd witnessed the total destruction of her home, her family, everything she had known, and if Alexander was correct, the entity that had been unleashed on this night had the potential to destroy so much more. And what about the radiation poisoning? Why did a few old paintings and statues matter anyway?

Alexander glanced back but said nothing.

The edifice creaked and groaned all around them, the air filled with a sound like boulders being crushed together. Fiona felt off balance, a sensation that increased with each step forward. Although the debris-strewn corridors were flat, she felt like she was walking downhill, and that at any moment, she might fall forward. She saw that the others were having similar difficulty moving and asked Alexander about this.

"It's the gravity of the black hole," Alexander explained. "Its mass is still relatively small right now, but as we draw closer, this effect will become more pronounced."

"It's still here? I thought that thing...the basilisk...was the black hole."

He shook his head. "Merely an extension of its presence. A drone, if you will. The black hole itself cannot move, though as it consumes more and more matter, its mass will increase until it sinks to the center of the Earth. When that happens..." He didn't finish the thought.

"How long will that take?" Sara asked.

"It is impossible to say. This is unexplored territory. The increase in its mass is not mathematically related to the amount of matter it consumes. But I fear that the time remaining might be measured in hours, not days or months."

"Hours?"

"The strange matter at the core of the singularity can add mass to any particle. Right now, it has a relatively limited supply—pieces of masonry, wood and plaster that have broken loose and fallen into the event horizon. Seventeen hundred years ago, something similar happened. The black hole was in a cave. It had consumed all the loose material nearby, after which, it could only draw away subatomic particles from the solid rock surrounding it, which is a very slow process. Relatively speaking, of course.

"But there is another source of material that might accelerate the process, one that was not available then. The sun. Sunlight is made up of particles that have very little mass. Some of these particles, neutrinos for example, are so small that they can pass through solid matter without striking other particles, sometimes penetrating many miles into the Earth's surface. When the black hole was in the cave, it was shielded from direct sunlight. Now, that is no longer the case. When the sun rises and light reaches the black hole, it will be showered by sub-atomic particles, all of which will be instantly converted into mass."

Fiona didn't understand the scientific principles he was trying to explain, but the bottom line was clear. When the sun rose, the world would end. "Can we really stop this thing?" she asked in a small voice.

Alexander clapped a firm hand on her shoulder. "I believe so. Those Buddhist monks found a way, centuries ago, and they didn't even know what they were dealing with."

"Maybe it's different this time," Sara suggested. "You were playing that recording of the chant they used, but it didn't seem to make any difference."

"That is true," Alexander conceded. "But I think that Fiona's experience may hold the key to that mystery. Recall how she was able to discern the mother tongue's influence in the original works of art, and even in the fragments of the Buddha statues, but not in reproductions."

"Copies don't work," Fiona said. "Has to be the real thing."

He nodded. "There is some deeper mystery at work. I was mistaken in believing that it was simply a matter of finding the right harmonic frequency. That was only part of it. Intention also plays a role. It was the intention of those monks, seventeen hundred years ago, to render the black hole dormant. And I believe that you can do the same, Fiona."

"Are you actually serious?" Julia said from behind them. "What you're proposing...it's like faith-healing. Believe and you'll be saved. Seriously? The real world doesn't work like that."

Alexander regarded her with a grim look that was almost menacing. "You are mistaken, Dr. Preston, and your skepticism isn't helping. Scientists have long recognized that intention—what you would call 'faith'—can influence the physical world. It is a precept of quantum mechanics, and that is exactly what we are dealing with here."

Despite Alexander's confident assurance, Julia's doubts weighed on Fiona. Did the fate of the world really depend on her ability to believe that she could save it? She took another step forward, and felt the inexorable attraction of the black hole, an invisible presence only a few hundred feet away, and knew that her faith was about to be put to the ultimate test.

37.

They marched like the professional soldiers they were, picking their way deftly over the uneven surface of the fractured road, maneuvering around abandoned vehicles and other obstacles without breaking stride. Suvorov led the way. Brown, either unable or unwilling to move with the same urgency, was being dragged along by two of the Spetsnaz.

King easily kept pace with them but did not allow the apparent truce to lull him into complacency. This was an alliance of convenience, and he did not doubt that, when or if they succeeded in dealing with the immediate crisis, the Russians would turn on him.

One thing at a time, he told himself.

They reached their destination only a few minutes later. The Louvre now bore little resemblance to the stately seventeenth century palace that had been transformed into what was arguably the most famous museum in the world. The classical façade had been devastated by the earthquake, particularly in the central part of the structure, which appeared to be on the verge of imploding. The towering pavilion had collapsed in on itself and the exterior walls, what little remained of them, leaned dangerously inward. In the foreground, little remained of the famous glass pyramids; the largest of the triangular structures now appeared to be nothing more than a twisted web of steel.

Suvorov had paused at the edge of the courtyard and was gazing in disbelief at the scene of near total destruction. "I can't believe it," he whispered, barely restraining his grief. "I was just here. A few hours ago."

King surveyed the ruin. The Russian had been right about the connection between the Buddha statues—or rather their remains—and the cause of the event. This had almost certainly been ground zero. Something powerful had been awakened inside the museum, and even though he was still more than a hundred yards from the structure, he knew it was still there. He could hear it in the persistent crunching sound that emanated from the ruins, and he could feel it in every fiber of his body.

The Russian quickly overcame his shock and led the group into the courtyard. He directed one of his team to remain outside and signal with a gun shot if and when the dark shape pursuing them finally arrived. King didn't doubt that it would show up, but he was starting to believe that what lay inside the museum might be even more dangerous. His dread, and an increasing sensation of vertigo, intensified with each step forward, and as they crawled through a gap in the museum's exterior and into its lightless depths, he felt almost like he was in free fall.

Suvorov's familiarity with the museum counted for little once they were inside. The labyrinth of corridors connecting the galleries and exhibition halls as shown on the floor plan had been remade by the temblor. Hallways were now blocked with rubble, while new passages had been created by the collapse of walls. There was no question however, as to the path they were to follow; gravity drew them irresistibly toward the center of the museum.

King saw nothing even faintly recognizable, but he knew

that the heaps of stone and masonry probably concealed price-less and irreplaceable objets d'art, now damaged beyond any hope of recovery. The clumps of debris had all accumulated on the inward facing walls—at least where such walls were still standing.

Then, after only a few minutes, the meandering journey ended at the edge of a crater, more than a hundred yards across and open to the night sky. Flashlight beams probed the down-ward slope, revealing openings that led into ancient passageways—remnants of the twelfth century fortress upon which the palace had been built—cutting into the bedrock that was itself scoured clean of any debris left over from the collapse of the roof and the floors above.

The bottom of the crater however was filled with loose fragments of rock and rubble, a heap several yards in diameter, and as King stared at the accumulation, he realized that it was the source of the ominous grinding sound.

He didn't know what the monster on the riverboat had been, but this surely was the black hole Pradesh had awakened.

The mound—what scientists called an 'accretion disk'—was moving, the fragments were being pulled inward, com-pacted together and broken into smaller pieces by the force of gravity, and all occurring at different relativistic speeds as the matter approached and ultimately crossed the event horizon. Black holes could not be seen because their gravity was too strong to allow light to reflect back to an observer but an accre-tion disk was a pretty good indicator of the presence of a black hole. King recalled that the destruction of matter in a black hole also released gamma radiation, which could cause lethal cell damage in humans. That wasn't something he wanted to think about.

Then he saw something else revealed in the glow of the flashlights. A group of people stood on the edge of the crater, about thirty yards away, similarly gazing down into its depths.

He recognized one figure immediately, the tall, massive form of Alexander Diotrophes—the immortal Hercules himself—squinting into the glare.

This revelation was accompanied by equal parts anger and hope. *Of course he's here*, King thought. *He always seems to turn up when the world's about to end. He probably saw this coming, but was too damn secretive to share what he knew with the rest of us.*

On the other hand, there wasn't much that Diotrophes didn't know. If there *was* a way to stop this thing, Alexander would be able to tell him how.

Then he saw the faces of Alexander's companions. His heart sank as a joyful squeal echoed from the walls of the crater.

"Dad!"

38.

Somehow, Julia wasn't a bit surprised by the appearance of the man Fiona identified as her father. She was not surprised to learn that the man, introducing himself simply as 'King' was also Sara's boyfriend, nor did she have any difficulty accepting that King and Carutius were old acquaintances—she didn't think they were friends exactly, but there was history there. She felt like she had lost her capacity to be surprised by anything where Carutius was involved.

But her mind still boggled with the revelation that the man she had met earlier, the man who had identified himself as 'Trevor,' was in fact Timur Suvorov, a Russian special forces soldier. That was too much.

Trevor—*Timur*, she corrected—did not allow the awkwardness of the situation to put down roots. "I will explain everything later," he told her. "But right now time is short."

"No kidding," Fiona chirped, and then with what could only be described as youthful enthusiasm, she summarized everything that had happened, starting with following Carutius—whom she kept calling Alexander—and leading up to the appearance of the dark shape.

"Basilisk," King muttered approvingly. "That sounds like a good name for it. We ran into it as well."

"The basilisk," Alexander said, "is merely an extension of the black hole's consciousness. The real danger is there." He pointed out to the accretion disk in the center of the crater.

"I'm not so sure," King countered. He held up something that looked to Julia like an ordinary cell phone. "This is a quantum computer. One of ten that Mr. Brown over there—" He pointed to an older man who was being held at gunpoint by one of Timur's companions—"was going to use to sabotage the world's power supply. The man who actually built the things had other plans. He somehow found a way to remotely wake up the black hole down there with the quantum computer network and evidently give it some brainpower. I think it wants to make that connection permanent, so it has that basilisk running around collecting them all. This is probably the last one, and if it gets it, we're finished."

Alexander considered this a moment. "Perhaps not. This may be a unique opportunity. If it possesses true intelligence, we might be able to interact with it…"

He let the thought trail off before any of the others could voice an objection. "No. There's no time. We need to act against this entity, just as the Buddhist monks did centuries ago."

"I can do it," Fiona said. "I'm going to use the mother tongue."

Julia noted the look of apprehension that crossed King's face. Before he could respond, the noise of a gunshot reached their ears. Several more followed in short bursts then fell silent.

King looked away for a moment, then bent forward and embraced Fiona. "You can do this," he told her, and then he drew back and spoke to Alexander. "The basilisk is here. I have to go."

The entity knew that its awareness was almost complete, and while it did not yet understand the subtleties of such intangible realities, it experienced satisfaction. The manifestation had collected all but one of the fractured pieces of its consciousness, and the last remaining piece had, quite inexplicably, been drawn near to the source—to the entity itself.

Its new awareness had increased the entity's knowledge of its physical environment. It knew that the manifestation was outside the building, and that it needed to go inside, *but the way was blocked by a wall. That posed no great difficulty; with a touch, the manifestation could change the mass of the obstacle, transforming it into a gaseous vapor. But as it reached out to open a passage, it felt again the impact of an assault.*

Bullets, *fired from* a gun.

This had happened before, when its understanding was not complete. Now, as then, the bullets could not harm it. As they touched the manifestation, the projectiles were changed, but this simple action caused the manifestation to halt its advance, if ever so slightly. These bullets...the gun that fired them...were keeping the manifestation from accomplishing its purpose, and that was intolerable.

Though it did not understand the subtleties of intangible realities, the entity experienced annoyance.

It reached out with its awareness. The bullets...the gun...a man.

The manifestation changed the man.

The assault ended. The entity experienced satisfaction. The manifestation returned to its purpose and began moving again.

39.

King drew away from Fiona and Sara and turned to Suvorov. He didn't know what to make of the Spetsnaz. Was he the Russian's captive? His partner?

"I've got to get moving," he said.

Suvorov nodded. "We'll try to slow it down."

King started to move away, but the Russian called out to him.

"Wait." He handed King the suppressed Uzi and the satchel full of magazines and improvised explosive devices. "Might come in handy."

King wasn't so sure about the sentiment, but was grateful for the gesture. He slung the satchel over a shoulder and then without further delay, set out along the perimeter of the crater, all the while feeling irresistibly drawn toward its center.

He knew that he had to stay ahead of the thing, but also that he had to draw it away from the others, because even a glancing contact would prove instantly fatal. Getting back outside the museum seemed his best course of action, but doing so would be a challenge, as the quake had collapsed hallways and blocked points of egress. A single wrong turn might send him to a dead end in a very literal sense.

Multiple reports—the Spetsnaz's Uzis and Chesler's pistol—reached his ears over the insistent grinding from the accretion disk, signaling that the dark shape, Fiona's *basilisk*, had arrived. He risked a glance back and saw the thing emerging at the edge of the pit, not far from the passage he and the Russians had used. But the basilisk didn't need to negotiate the choked corridors of the museum; it had passed right through all obstacles in its path.

The muzzle flash from the guns illuminated the surreal skirmish like strobe lights, revealing the scene in a series of freeze-frame images. The basilisk barely moved as bullets poured into it. Suvorov had been right about being able to slow it down, but he didn't dare believe that it was possible to harm this otherworldly thing. Indeed, despite the hesitation, the great dark shape appeared to shrug off the fusillade and began sliding forward, creeping out over the edge of the pit, angling straight toward King.

King realized immediately that the basilisk was unaffected by the micro black hole's gravity well, and felt panic rise in his chest. The basilisk would be able to cut across the crater and quickly close the intervening distance while he was reduced to practically crawling along the precarious edge of the pit.

Damn. I should have expected that.

He reached an opening leading back into the museum, and reluctantly climbed inside. He caught one last glimpse of the others—of Sara, Fiona and Alexander huddled together in preparation to do whatever it was they were going to do to stop the black hole—and he breathed a silent prayer that they would succeed. Then he ventured into the dark tunnel.

40.

The explosive report of gunfire made Fiona jump, but Alexander's firm hand on her shoulder calmed her nerves. She gazed up at him. "Tell me what to do."

"Do you recall the sound from the recording I was playing? 'Om.' It is an ancient word, the first part of the Buddhist mantra, which when chanted, clears the meditative mind and opens one's awareness to the universe. The word likely derives from the mother tongue and is full of power."

"If it's that simple," Sara asked, making no effort to hide her anxiety, "why do you need Fiona to do it?"

"Last time, it took the combined voices of an entire village to render the black hole dormant, and even then, it was a close thing. They repeated the word, but did not understand it. It is my belief...my hope, that Fiona's ability to understand the mother tongue will make the difference." He turned his attention again to the girl. "The word might be only the beginning. As you speak it, open your mind to what you know of the mother tongue. The knowledge is in you. Your ability to recognize the hidden language of creation in works of art proves it, and if you can unlock that knowledge, you will be able to bend the black hole to your will, even as you once used it to stop the golem."

"Bend it?"

"Tell it what to do. Black holes are so much more than just destroyers. They are gateways to other realities, gateways that are closed to us because of our own physical limitations. You hold the key to changing that, Fiona."

"I just want to stop it."

"And so you shall. But you must trust me, and follow my instructions no matter how difficult it seems." He grasped her hands and directed her to sit on the floor. He sat in front of her, crossing his legs in the yogic lotus position, but bracing her against the inexorable pull of the black hole's gravity. "Now, let us begin."

"Can I help?" Sara asked, likewise settling down next to Fiona.

Alexander nodded then drew in a deep breath, indicating that they should do the same.

Fiona felt her chest grow tight with fear. What if she couldn't do this? What if Alexander was wrong and she didn't know how to tell the black hole what to do? King would die…they would all die.

But if Alexander was right about the radiation poisoning, they were all dead already. So what difference did it make?

With her lungs filled like a balloon about to burst, Fiona pressed her lips together and let the strange word vibrate from the roof of her mouth.

"Om."

41.

Fickle luck decided to throw King a bone. In addition to being broad and relatively intact, the passage was lit at intervals by battery-operated emergency lights and exit signs. He sprinted down the corridor, glancing back every few seconds to see if the basilisk was following. The third time he did this, he saw that it was.

The thing was a moving wall of darkness, filling the height and breadth of the hallway, rolling forward like a ponderous but unstoppable tsunami of night. One by one, the emergency lights were engulfed in its mass and the scant illumination behind King dimmed.

He put on a fresh burst of speed, taking a left turn at an intersection—as indicated by the arrow on the exit sign—without slowing, and once again, briefly lost sight of the basilisk.

A few more turns brought him to the exit, or rather the place where the exit door had been. Now, there was just a gaping hole where the entire wall had collapsed inward. He picked his way across the rubble, painfully aware that the delay was erasing his lead, and vaulted through the opening into the night.

Muted light issued from the breach in the wall, and as he ran out across the courtyard, he glanced back, waiting for the moment that the light would be eclipsed by the basilisk's bulk.

Several seconds passed, but the light did not change.

Something was wrong. The basilisk wasn't following him anymore.

King felt a new rush of fear as the realization hit home. If it wasn't chasing him, that could only mean…

"Fiona!"

The entity had no memory of its past, but it comprehended this new threat.

The manifestation had nearly reached the man who carried the last fragment of its consciousness, but that was no longer the entity's primary concern. The word resonated through every particle of its physical being and it understood what would happen if the speaker of the word was not immediately silenced.

The entity was not defenseless. The word stimulated it in a way that the creatures of this world would understand as pain, and just as pain triggered a violent, instinctive reaction in those fragile beings of flesh, so too did the harmonic vibrations cause the entity's essence to respond with furious intensity.

Raw matter spiraled into the entity and was changed. Its mass increased…doubled…and doubled again.

The steady hum of the word faltered as the world around the entity shook, but the reprieve was short-lived. The speaking resumed and the pain returned.

Though it did not understand the subtleties of intangible realities, the entity experienced fear.

Filled with primal desperation, the entity turned the manifestation away from its pursuit and summoned it back with a new purpose.

42.

As a vibration rumbled up through the ground, Suvorov threw his arms around Julia and tackled her to the ground. The reaction was instinctive. He barely knew the woman and she meant nothing at all to him, but protecting her felt like the most natural thing in the world.

He'd felt the same way about assisting King. Despite the fact that the man was notionally the enemy of his country, despite the fact that King had killed Kharitonov, Suvorov knew that King was motivated by something profoundly superior to patriotism or a desire for revenge. King was risking himself to help others, to save a world of strangers, and that was something Suvorov could not help but admire.

He had emptied two magazines into the basilisk before it disappeared into the passage after King. The bullets had definitely slowed the thing down, and that made him think that it might be possible to kill it. It would surely take more rounds than they had, but he wasn't going to let that fact prevent him from taking action.

Then the quake had started.

He covered Julia with his own body as the walls of the

Louvre groaned under the increasingly violent shaking. The earlier tremor had already collapsed the roof overhead, eliminating the danger of anything falling on them, but now pieces of debris were breaking off and falling at an angle, like raindrops being driven sideways by a fierce wind. Suvorov felt chunks of marble and wood strike his exposed back before bouncing away and tumbling into the pit. Then he felt Julia and himself sliding into the crater as well.

He frantically scrambled for a purchase and his fingers curled around a piece of metal jutting from the wall of the crater.

Pain tore through him. He felt as if his left arm had been wrenched from its socket. It was not just the combination of his own weight with Julia's; he felt impossibly heavy, like his clothes were made of lead. Julia, her arms wrapped tightly around his waist, seemed to weigh a ton, and he could feel her slipping.

A scream pierced the ominous rumble and Suvorov glimpsed his teammate, Konstantin Vasileyev, tumbling down the side of the pit. The Spetsnaz's fingers clawed at the rough slope of the crater but to no avail. Vasileyev slammed into the slowly gyrating mass of debris at the center and was smashed flat against it like an insect against the canopy of a fighter jet.

Suvorov thrust the horror of his comrade's demise from his mind and focused on saving himself and Julia. He wrapped his legs around her, squeezing tight to prevent her from slipping further, and then released the embrace of his right arm and reached for the metal protrusion.

Ignoring the agony in his left shoulder, he heaved with all his might. A sustained exertion got him only a few inches before exhaustion forced him to relent, but thankfully, the sloping crater wall afforded enough resistance to keep them from sliding back. After a few seconds of respite, he tried again.

The ceaseless ordeal seemed to drag on forever, though in

reality it took only about a minute. As soon as he got his upper torso level with the protrusion, he was able to heave Julia up and over the lip of the crater. The black hole's gravity still tugged at him, like sandbags tied around his ankles, but without the additional burden of Julia, he was able to scramble the remaining distance to join her on the flat ground at the pit's edge.

The earth still shook beneath them and pieces of rubble peppered them like hailstones, but through it all he could hear a faint humming—Fiona, Alexander and Sara, clinging together precariously at the edge of the crater, but still sounding the atonal chant that would, if the big man was to be believed, render the black hole dormant.

A series of loud reports alerted him to a new danger. Chesler, about twenty yards away and clinging with one hand to an upright column, was firing his pistol into the shadows.

No, not shadows, Suvorov realized. *The basilisk.*

He could barely make out the dark shape as it slid from the ruins of the museum and began oozing along the crater rim.

It got King and now it's coming back for the rest of us, he thought.

The basilisk seemed to recoil from the impact of Chesler's rounds. Suvorov felt sure he could sense its frantic need to advance, and suddenly he understood. The quake had started at almost exactly the same moment that Fiona and the others had begun to chant. The black hole knew what they were doing and was desperate to stop them.

Chesler's pistol clicked empty and he hastily hit the release and let the spent magazine fall. The metal arced away at an impossible angle and bounced down the side of the crater. Chesler fumbled another magazine from his shoulder holster, but before he could insert it into the pistol grip, a dark tentacle snaked toward him.

Suvorov grimaced as the SVR operative was vaporized. The

chant was working, but if the basilisk reached Fiona and the others, all would be lost. And he was the only one left who could stop it.

The basilisk resumed its advance, now only ten yards away.

Bullets wouldn't be enough, he realized. They might slow it down, but he didn't have enough rounds to keep it pinned down indefinitely. No, he knew what he would have to do to stop it.

He threw back the flap on his satchel and reached in. His fingers closed around one of the IED's, but he did not draw it out. It was one of the flash-bangs they had improvised, but that wouldn't make a difference for what he had in mind. When the device detonated, it would set off the rest—nearly five pounds of Semtex altogether.

Five yards away now, and only about thirty yards from where Fiona desperately tried to keep up the chant. *Too close*, he thought, and he knew exactly what he was going to have to do.

As a soldier, he had always been ready to give his life in defense of his country. But what did that even mean? How many brave men—men like his blood brother Ian Kharitonov—had died, not protecting their fellow citizens from invaders, but simply to advance the interests of a privileged few, for mere political or economic gains?

Suvorov was about to give his life to save the world. How often did a chance like that come along?

He activated the timer and shouted, "Julia, stay down!"

Then he turned to basilisk and smiled.

He caught a flicker of movement as a dark tendril lashed out at him, and then saw no more.

43.

As King dashed back into the Louvre, the earth began to move beneath his feet. He careened back down the tunnel, but the violent shaking sent him bouncing off the walls. Chunks of debris fell from overhead to land directly in his path. A few pieces struck him, knocking him flat, but thankfully none were large enough to pin him down or cause unconsciousness.

He reached the edge of the crater just in time to see Chesler evaporate. The man's abrupt demise sent a shudder through him. He'd witnessed every manner of death and knew that rarely was the final passing ever truly instantaneous. He had always wondered if death would be like that old Ambrose Bierce story, where the final moments of consciousness stretched out into a wondrous dream. But what went through your mind when every atom of your body came apart in a nanosecond?

King ventured out into the crater, and immediately felt the black hole's gravity pulling at him. It was much stronger now; at least as powerful as the G force he felt when Chess Team's supersonic stealth plane, *Crescent*, took off. The difference here was that instead of being pushed back into an acceleration seat, the force here was trying to yank him off his feet and into the crater. He leaned into the wall and, with as much speed as he could muster, headed out after the basilisk, but even as he did, he knew he wasn't going to make it in time.

He hauled the Uzi around and took aim. Maybe he could distract the thing, get it to come after him the way it had Chesler, and give Fiona a few more seconds.

The basilisk filled the Uzi's sights, but in the corner of his eye, he saw Suvorov make a move. Even from a distance, he could see what the Russian was about to do, and threw him a mental salute as he waited for explosive package to detonate.

The Russian disappeared from view but after a few seconds, the dark shape advanced again, and King saw Suvorov standing motionless with the satchel still clutched in his hands. The Spetsnaz leader did not move. The IEDs in the satchel did not explode, and King knew with sickening certainty the man and the devices had been transformed into stone.

Now nothing at all stood between the basilisk and Fiona.

King pulled the trigger on the Uzi. The suppressor muted the violence of the discharge, but a stream of lead arced out across the crater and vanished into the basilisk's bulk. "Come on," he shouted as the bolt slid forward against the last spent cartridge. "You wanted me, remember?"

The basilisk ignored him and oozed ever closer to Fiona and the others.

If it gets to her, we're all finished. There was only one way he could think of to save Fiona.

He let the useless pistol fall, not even noticing as it was pulled away in the gravity storm, and cupped his hands around his mouth. "Fiona!" he shouted at the top of his lungs. "Stop!"

44.

Through the earthquake, Fiona had managed to keep up the chant, but it seemed like all they were accomplishing was to really piss off the black hole. Now the basilisk was heading their way.

She concentrated on uttering the mantra, but fear stole her breath and she could only manage a few seconds of humming with each inhalation. Alexander's hand gripped her arm, a forceful but silent exhortation to ignore the threat and stay focused, but she knew it wasn't going to work. The basilisk was going to kill them all.

And then King's voice reached out to her, telling her to stop.

She did.

"No Fiona," Alexander rasped. "You must keep going. It's the only way."

Sara fell silent as well and then hugged Fiona protectively, as if silently encouraging her to trust her decision in the face of Alexander's growing rage.

"You must keep going," Alexander repeated urgently, "Or all will be lost."

Fiona felt her heart torn in two. Alexander knew what he was talking about; he'd stopped the black hole once before. But she trusted King implicitly, and if he said to stop... But what if he was wrong?

The basilisk halted its advance, shadowy tentacles poised mere inches from where they sat. Fiona wanted to retreat from it, but her limbs were leaden and the ground was still shaking violently beneath her. She feared that any attempt to move might send her plunging into the crater.

King's voice continued to reach out across the ominous grinding noise of the debris shifting into the black hole and the groan of the Louvre coming apart all around them, but he wasn't talking to Fiona anymore. He held up a phone and waved it. "This is what you want, you bastard. Right here. Come and get it."

Fiona wasn't sure she could trust what she was seeing; the basilisk was moving away.

"Now," Alexander roared. "It's leaving. We must resume the mantra."

"No." The word was barely audible, a timid breath that seemed to falter before she could get it past her lips. She gathered her courage and tried again. "No. King said to stop. He knows what he's doing."

"He knows nothing!" Alexander's rage was as overpowering as the black hole itself.

Fiona hugged Sara tighter, and when she spoke, her words were directed only at herself. "I believe in him."

For a fleeting second, she thought Alexander's anger might turn physical. But if such was ever his intent, he didn't get a chance to act, for at that moment, a section of wall broke free behind them and sailed toward the black hole like a kite caught in a gale force wind. Fiona caught just a glimpse of it before it slammed into all three of them, sweeping them toward oblivion.

When the word ceased to be spoken, the speaker winked out of the entity's awareness. Without the word to guide it, the manifestation halted, poised to act the instant the sound resumed and all the while aware of the close proximity of the remaining fragment of the consciousness.

The entity waited. Its consciousness, incomplete though it was, understood the causal nature of the world it now inhabited. It understood what would happen if the word continued to be spoken, and it understood that the speaker of the word intended exactly that outcome.

Why then had the speaking stopped?

The entity could not comprehend this, and was, for a few brief nanoseconds, caught in an endless logic loop. Failing to find an explanation for the cessation of the word, the entity returned the manifestation to its original purpose. Perhaps all would be clear when the final piece of its consciousness was added.

The manifestation moved immediately for its original goal and reached out with a finger of its strange essence. It embraced the item that contained the last fragment without changing it, and immediately as it made contact, the entity's sense of satisfaction multiplied. With the assimilation of the final piece, its mind was made complete.

Now, there remained but one final task for the manifestation: return the complete mind to the entity. The entity's awesome power to change the very fabric of reality would be joined to the limitless possibilities of awareness...of thought.

Though it did not grasp that ancient villagers had once thought it to be a devil, the entity now understood that it had become what the insignificant inhabitants of this world would call a god.

45.

King remained motionless in the face of the basilisk's advance. It seemed to be moving faster now, but that was probably just an illusion caused by the fact that it was coming straight at him. Even if he had wanted to flee, it would have been impossible with the black hole's gravity exerting an almost irresistible pull that threatened to send him tumbling down into the crater.

He watched as a tendril reached out for the satchel where he'd stashed the quantum phone. If Brown's supposition about the importance of a connection to a human user was correct, then the basilisk would be coming for him next, but that was a sacrifice he was willing to make to give Fiona a chance to finish what she needed to do.

The quantum phone disappeared into the basilisk's massive form, and then without a moment's pause, it shifted course and descended into the pit, toward the accretion disk.

King waited, not daring to breathe. He had just given the black hole the one thing it wanted most; if this gamble failed, there was no telling what the consequences of that decision would be.

The basilisk reached the swirling rubble pile and then, as if it were no more substantial than smoke or shadow, seeped into the grinding rock mass.

Then something strange happened. There wasn't a flash or an explosion or any other kind of display, but the change was just as instantaneous. The mass lurched a little, as if the accretion disk had hiccupped, and shimmered in the dim light as the swirling pieces of rubble and debris were pulverized into particles finer than sand. Then the entire mass appeared to implode, shrinking inward as if sucked through a straw into another dimension.

For a fleeting instant, King thought his plan had worked. When the basilisk had grabbed the satchel with the quantum phone, it had also taken about five pounds of Semtex, wired to a detonator which he'd set with a ten-second delay.

Suvorov had given him the idea. The Russian had observed the effect of bullets on the thing and had sacrificed himself in a futile effort to get explosives close enough to do some real damage. Unfortunately, the basilisk's touch had altered the chemical nature of the plastique, rendering it completely inert.

But Suvorov's idea had been a good one. King had gambled on the fact that within the monster's impenetrable body, the quantum phones were still intact, and that it would add his phone to the collection, along with his ticking time bomb.

Beyond that, he hadn't known what to expect. He didn't know if the basilisk could be damaged; maybe it could absorb the energy and shrapnel as effectively as it absorbed bullets. He was hoping that, at the very least, the blast would completely destroy the quantum phones. When the basilisk had gone into the accretion disk, he had dared to hope that it might somehow be enough to destroy the black hole itself. Instead, the energy of the explosion, compressed and amplified by the black hole's gravity, had liquefied the accretion disk, allowing the entire mass of debris to be instantly consumed by the singularity.

King wondered if he had just made things a hell of a lot

worse. He could still feel the black hole's gravity, stronger now than before. He couldn't tell what was happening at the center of the pit; it roiled in his vision like convection waves off hot asphalt.

At least the basilisk seemed to be gone. Now it was up to Fiona to save the day. He turned away from the crater and searched for Fiona and the others...

His heart seized in his chest as he tried to comprehend what he was seeing. A massive piece of rubble—a section of wall or ceiling—had crashed down right where they had been seated. Alexander was still there, his head and arms protruding out from beneath the slab and out over the edge of the pit. Fiona and Sara had both been swept over the edge. Alexander had caught them, but it was evident from the strain on his face that he couldn't hold on much longer.

King started crawling toward them. He didn't dare try to stand; if he raised his center of gravity, he would surely topple over and fall into the black hole. Even now, pressed flat against the ground, he felt like he was slipping sideways.

King was only about ten feet from Alexander when something slammed into his ribs. As he slid into the pit, King caught a glimpse of a gloating Graham Brown, staring down at him.

46.

Once they'd discovered the black hole inside the Louvre, both King and the Russians had completely lost interest in Brown. He could have slipped away at any time, and several times, he almost did.

But what good would that have done?

This wasn't the first time he'd lost big; nobody could climb as high as he had, without getting knocked back down a few times. He'd always come back, stronger than ever.

Not this time.

He couldn't believe how badly he'd misjudged Pradesh. He was an excellent judge of character, and the Indian computer expert had never struck him as anything more than an opportunistic cyber-mercenary. He never would have believed that the man harbored apocalyptic delusions, much less the technical know-how to use the quantum computer to summon a black hole out of thin air.

But that was exactly what Pradesh, with Brown's unwitting help, had done. Pradesh had started a wildfire that would devour everything, and there wasn't a thing anyone could do to stop it.

So why bother trying to escape?

His only regret was that he wouldn't be going out a winner, and when he spied King crawling along the edge of the crater, he saw a chance for one last victory. Again and again, this man had beaten him, thwarting his carefully laid plans. Now, it was time for payback.

His first kick caught King completely unaware, and sent him sliding toward the edge. Brown hugged the ground to avoid being dislodged from his own precarious position, then drew back his foot and kicked again, driving his heel toward King's face.

He missed. King ducked away from the attack, and then threw one arm around the gambler's outstretched foot. King's weight stretched Brown's leg like a hangman's rope. The gambler grimaced in unexpected agony as his knee and hip joints hyper-extended with a sucking noise. King felt impossibly heavy. Brown clutched at the ground, but found nothing to grasp. The heels of his palms skidded futilely on the rough ground as he slid toward the crater, with King desperately trying to pull him down…

No, he realized. *He's trying to pull himself back up.*

Through his agony, Brown felt a sudden thrill of understanding. Why was he fighting this? They were both dead men anyway; by struggling against his fate, he was really accomplishing nothing more than to give King another chance to beat him.

In fact, the probability was quite high that if he managed to endure this, King would survive—albeit temporarily—and exact his own retribution against Brown. The only way to win this game was to be in control at the very end, and so, with something almost like a smile, he stopped fighting and launched himself toward the pit.

One final time, King defied Brown's expectations. Perhaps anticipating that Brown would opt for a pyrrhic victory, he had spent those desperate moments securing a handhold, and when

Brown let go, so did King.

The black hole's gravity caught Brown instantly. He slammed against the side of the crater and tumbled uncontrollably down the slope like someone being dragged behind a speeding car.

And then he stopped.

47.

King pressed himself flat against the ground, trying to create as much friction as he could to keep from following Brown into the black hole. His legs and lower torso still dangled out over the precipice. He didn't know whether the gambler had thrown himself in or simply fallen, but from the moment he'd managed to snare Brown's leg, he'd known that his survival would depend on finding something else to hold onto.

In his peripheral vision, he'd glimpsed Brown's arrival at the event horizon of the micro black hole. The gambler's plunge seemed to slow as he neared the bottom of the crater, coming to an almost complete stop, suspended in mid air right above the roiling distortion that concealed the black hole. Brown's agonized face gazed up from the pit, an expression of profound disappointment fixed there as if sculpted in bronze. His legs and lower torso, much closer to the center, appeared to stretch, as if made of taffy, and swirled into the nothingness.

King thought about what Pradesh had said earlier. *You experience infinity...like being one with the mind of God.*

I wonder what Brown's infinity looks like.

He turned away, knowing that he was one wrong move

away from sharing Brown's fate. Unfortunately, there didn't seem to be any right moves. Then he felt a hand close on his outstretched arm.

It was Julia. Her face was a twisted mask of fear and exhaustion, but her grip on his wrist was fierce, determined. She certainly wasn't strong enough to pull him back, nor did she weigh enough to anchor him, but he could see that she wasn't about to let go. He gave her a nod of encouragement, and then, trusting in her resolve, he took a chance.

On his first try, he managed to scoot forward just an inch, but it was progress. He tried again and succeeded in getting his thighs up onto solid ground, and after that, he was able to extricate himself in short order. As soon as he was moving unaided, Julia shrank back, away from the edge, and pressed herself against a section of stone wall. King realized that he knew nothing about this woman that had just come to his aid; he wondered if he would ever get a chance to change that.

Fiona and Sara still dangled from Alexander's outstretched arm. How long had they been there? A few seconds? Minutes? Alexander's strength was literally the stuff of legend, but even demigods had their limitations. And if the mythic Hercules wasn't strong enough to pull them back from the brink, what could he hope to accomplish? The simple truth was that pulling his loved ones from danger was beyond his ability. So what did that leave?

He was moving again before he had an answer, crawling to where Alexander still lay pinned and almost completely spent, but he did not stop there. Instead, he kept going, out over the edge. He moved with the practiced caution of a veteran climber, picking out handholds, wedging hands and feet into cracks. His limbs felt like molten lead, and every maneuver required an extraordinary exertion, but his destination was close.

"Sara!" He called out, and then, "Fiona! I'm here."

48.

Fiona, wide-eyed with fear, looked at him and opened her mouth. The black hole's gravity was making it impossible for her to breathe. She tried to shout back at him, a plea for help, but what came out was a barely audible squeak.

King held her gaze. "Fi. Remember what you were trying to do? The mother tongue? Singing this thing a lullaby? You have to keep doing it. You're the only one who can."

She gave her head a quick shake, fearful that any movement might dislodge her from her precarious position and send her plummeting into the black hole. "Can't," she mouthed.

"Yes, you can."

"I don't know what to say." This time, she got words out in a hoarse whisper.

"You do know," King insisted. "You just don't know that you know. Start talking, start singing. It will come to you."

"He's right, Fi," Sara said, whispering into her ear. "The words don't even matter..."

Despite her own looming death, Fiona could not help but smile as she finished Sara's statement: "It's the thought that counts."

But wasn't that the truth? Alexander's recordings had used the correct word, the precise frequency that should have prevented the black hole from reawakening, but it hadn't worked because the words weren't coupled to a specific intention.

She thought back to the words she had spoken to stop Richard Ridley's golem; words in the ancient mother tongue, the language of creation, and wondered if her intention at that moment had been a source of greater power than the words themselves?

Those words would be of little use now. So also, she realized, was Alexander's Bhuddist mantra. That word was meaningless to her; how could she believe in the power of a word she didn't even understand?

But there was a language that she did know intimately, a language that had its roots in the ancient mother tongue, a language of which she was now the sole living guardian.

Fiona sucked in a breath against the crush of gravity, then freed one hand and began clapping it against her thigh, beating out a steady, insistent rhythm. Then, she began to sing.

49.

King didn't understand a word of what Fiona was saying, but recognized that it had to be her native language—the nearly extinct tongue of the Siletz tribe. The noises didn't even seem like words, just a string of vocalizations, but he could see the effect that they were having on the girl. The pain and fear had slipped from her face, replaced by a serene, almost confident expression.

King focused on what she was saying, and began to distinguish certain words that were repeated every few seconds like a refrain. He began to anticipate when she would utter the phrase, and gradually, haltingly at first, but then with more gusto, added his voice. He became aware that Sara was trying to harmonize as well.

"This is wrong," Alexander rasped from above. The words had to fight their way past clenched teeth. "You cannot control it this way. You must speak the word I taught you."

Fiona ignored him, but when King glanced up, he saw a strange fury building in the other man's eyes.

He wouldn't...

There wasn't time for King to finish the thought. He

threw his right arm out and embraced Fiona and Sara just as Alexander's grip failed.

There was simply no way he could hope to hang onto their combined weight or arrest their slide into the crater, but that didn't stop him from trying.

He shoved his free hand into a crack, braced his feet against protrusions on the cave wall, and pulled back with all his might.

It was like trying to pull a locomotive uphill. The shoulder of the arm that held the falling women burned; the muscles and tendons taut like a wire about to snap.

He felt his feet slip from their perch, then his hand was torn free and they were all sliding down the slope. It was not a free fall, not like it had been with Brown. The slope was about forty-five degrees but there were plenty of protruding surfaces to provide a little resistance in the form of painful friction. Nevertheless, the end result would be the same. Gravity owned them now, and the journey would not end until they reached the event horizon, where time would stand still and they would spend an eternity on the cusp of oblivion.

Through it all, Fiona kept singing, as did King.

After a few seconds passed, King realized that they were no longer sliding toward the event horizon. His efforts to find a handhold had paid off; the fingers of his left hand had wrapped around a protruding horn of rock. What surprised him though was that he had been able to maintain the grip, and he understood that the tidal force of gravity had, if only momentarily, abated.

Whatever Fiona was doing was working.

He noticed a change in her song, new and unfamiliar phrases issued from her mouth, and when he glanced down, he saw that she had stopped clapping out the rhythm and in fact had gone almost completely limp. Her eyes had rolled back in her head and the words that burbled from her lips were the mumblings of someone in a trance state.

King listened for a moment, trying to learn the refrain of this new mantra—it didn't sound like a Native American language anymore—but then a movement at the bottom of the crater arrested his attention.

Something was emerging from the event horizon.

King knew that what he was seeing could not really be happening. Nothing material could escape from the event horizon of a black hole. To do so would require acceleration to faster-than-light speeds—a physical impossibility—and would require more energy than existed in the entire universe. Impossibilities notwithstanding, there was a definite bulge in the visual distortion at the center of the crater.

The basilisk! King thought in a sudden panic. Maybe the explosion hadn't killed it after all. Maybe he'd failed to destroy the quantum computer network with the IED.

Suddenly, the event horizon erupted. It was not the black mass of the basilisk that burst forth, but rather a gray-brown column that shot like a geyser into the air above the crater. The crown of the plume was lost in the dark night, but in the space of a few seconds, King saw particles of fine dust precipitating from the cloud.

As the fallout intensified into a choking miasma, he hastily tugged free a shirttail and fashioned an impromptu mask as the gritty rain began to cloud his vision.

In the darkness that followed, he heard Fiona's voice, still speaking the strange language. Then, after a few minutes, she stopped, coughed twice, and fell silent.

50.

King pulled Fiona and Sara close. He could see them now, though just barely. It had taken nearly twenty minutes for most of the dust to settle, but the finest particulate would probably remain suspended in the air for hours. King didn't need to see the aftermath to know that the threat of the black hole was gone. The Earth had stopped shaking, there was no longer the sound of matter from the accretion disk being crushed into the event horizon, and the sense of disorientation and heaviness that had accompanied the alteration in gravity was gone.

King's mind burned with questions about what had happened, but for a few minutes, he was content to simply hug the pair—his family.

Twenty feet above them, Alexander gave a tremendous roar as he lifted the section of wall that had pinned him, and shoved it aside. Then, as if merely recovering from a stumble on the sidewalk, he brushed himself off and glissaded down into the crater where he greeted Fiona like she were a long lost relative.

"You did it, child!" He exclaimed. "When my grip failed, I feared all was lost, but you succeeded."

King managed to keep his expression neutral as he regarded the big man. There was something disingenuous about Alexander's praise.

He let them fall...but why? King shook his head. That didn't make any sense. He was allowing his natural distrust of Alexander Diotrophes make him paranoid.

"Tell me," Alexander continued. "How did you accomplish it? The language you were speaking...that was the Siletz dialect, was it not?"

Fiona nodded. "Dad told me to just start talking, and it came to me. I thought, if anything can stop this thing from destroying the world, it would be the story of the creation of the world. My grandmother taught it to me. Then I sang the healing blessing. As I said the words, I just kept telling myself to believe that everything would be fixed. That we would all be okay."

Alexander nodded approvingly and King detected no trace of deception in his dust-streaked face. King saw that Julia had also joined them on the side of the pit, and at the mention of 'healing,' she took something from her pocket and inspected it in the dim light. King saw that it was a film badge dosimeter, similar to the kind used on nuclear submarines to alert the wearer to possible exposure to dangerous levels of radiation.

The disk was uniformly white.

That surprised King. The destruction of matter at the event horizon of a black hole released intense gamma ray bursts, and it was believed that the effect would be even more pronounced with micro black holes. But the dosimeter had not changed color; apparently, they had dodged that bullet. Julia must have been thinking the same thing, because as she held the badge up for the others to see, they all broke into unfettered laughter.

The triumphant moment soon passed and King finally asked the question that was foremost in his mind. "Sara, what in

God's name are you and Fi doing here?"

Sara's story was only part of the greater chronicle of the night's events, and before long, Fiona and Julia...and even King himself, added to the narrative. Alexander offered a few insights, but discreetly avoided mentioning anything that might reveal his immortal nature to Julia. King however didn't bother with secrets. Julia had questions about Suvorov, and he felt the best way to honor the man's sacrifice was to tell her the truth.

"So what happened to the black hole?" King asked when all the stories were told. He directed this inquiry to Alexander who was inspecting the center of the crater.

Alexander blew grit away from a gritty stone—just another chunk of debris that had settled at the bottom of the crater. He held up the dark chunk of rubble, inspecting it. His face soured and then he seemed to notice that all eyes were on him. After a quick search of his memory, he shrugged and looked to Fiona for the answer. "Ask her."

The girl seemed surprised by the question and spread her hands in a gesture of ignorance. "How should I know?"

"It responded to you," Alexander supplied, brushing off his hands and standing up. "You took control of it. What did you tell it to do?"

"I don't remember telling it anything," Fiona said, but a thoughtful look came over her. "I remember though, when I was singing the creation story, I kept thinking how the black hole was the opposite of creation, and what the universe must have been like before the Old-Man-in-the-Sky made everything.

"I think maybe I told it to un-create itself," she finished, saying it almost like a question.

King recalled how Fiona had slipped into a trance-like state; whatever she had been saying during that time, it hadn't been her native Siletz language. "Well, it's gone now," he said, giving her another hug.

"It may be gone, but there's going to be a hell of a mess to clean up," Julia intoned. "How are we going to explain all this?"

"An earthquake," Alexander said. "Rare for this part of the world, but not unheard of. The seismological record will confirm that. As to the exact nature of the damage..." He shrugged.

"Why not just tell the truth?" Sara asked, matter-of-factly.

"That a crazy man managed to figure out a way to turn on a black hole?" King replied, a hint of good-natured sarcasm in his words. "And a teenaged girl sang it a lullaby, and saved the world."

"Well, when you put it that way..."

"An earthquake then," Julia agreed. "But how will we explain those?"

She pointed to the two towering objects that dominated the center of the crater. King had never seen these massive carvings, hadn't even seen pictures of them, but he had no trouble recognizing them.

Emerging from the spot that once been obscured by the event horizon of the black hole, and rising more than a hundred feet into the Parisian night above the ruins of the Louvre, untouched by the ravages of time and the intolerance of terrorists, stood the Bamiyan Buddhas.

EPILOGUE

Two days later

King stretched his legs out on the plush hotel bed—
appropriately, a king-sized mattress—and propped his head up
on a double-thickness of pillows. He could just make out the
sound of water running in the suite's bathroom, and while Sara
was showering, he decided to catch up on the latest news out of
Paris. She had firmly forbidden him from watching the nearly
constant coverage of the situation there, especially in Fiona's
presence, and King understood her reasoning. Fiona probably
felt a little like the biblical prophet Jonah—an unlucky magnet
for trouble on an epic scale—and the last thing she needed was
to be reminded of what they had gone through.

While the quake had rocked every corner of the city, most
of the structural damage was confined to the area around the
Louvre, and thankfully, the loss of life was minimal. And while
the former palace-turned-museum had suffered catastrophic
damage, only a few of the irreplaceable works of art had been
damaged beyond repair. Julia Preston would certainly be busy.
As curator-at-large for the Global Heritage Commission, she
would be instrumental in the effort to repair the damage done

to the Louvre. Restoration of the museum and the artwork, like the rebuilding of the city itself, would bring Parisians together in a unified effort, at least in the near term, just as the international relief effort—which had almost immediately been launched on various social networking platforms—was unifying the globe.

It's too bad, King thought, *that it always takes a tragedy to get people to work together.*

What was still not understood was the cause of the city-wide power outage, though some experts now believed that the quake had been part of an electro-magnetic event—not a full-blown magnetic pole reversal, but a definite polar hiccup. That theory was gaining popularity, particularly as it offered an explanation for the fact that almost all radio communications had been interrupted at the time of the quake. The phenomenon would also account for the fact that several helicopters and small planes had been knocked out of the sky. Nothing of course could explain the appearance of the fully formed Buddha statues, but that story was being kept out of the news.

King switched off the television. The real story would probably never become public knowledge, and he was just fine with that.

He was still troubled by the role Alexander Diotrophes had played in the events of that night. There was no question that the man's awareness of the micro black hole's existence and his knowledge of how it might be stopped had been pivotal in preventing a global cataclysm, but the very fact of his presence—right place, right time—made the hairs on the back of King's neck bristle with suspicion. It was almost as if the man had known that something was going to happen...as if he'd been waiting for it to happen.

And had he really let Fiona and Sara fall? Had that been intentional?

He shook his head, certain that he had misinterpreted the

look in Alexander's eyes. The big man had said all along that Fiona was the only one who could stop the black hole; what possible reason could he have had for letting her die?

He swung his legs off the bed and stood, crossing to the desk where he picked up the telephone and dialed a number. When an anonymous computerized switchboard began reciting a menu of options, he keyed in the code that would immediately connect him with Deep Blue.

"King!" The voice in his ear was both relieved and irritated. "Where have you been?"

"My phone got knocked out by whatever it was that hit Paris. This is the first chance I've had to check in." That was mostly true. He probably could have called sooner, but his first priority had been to get Fiona and Sara away from Paris. Given the disruption of infrastructure and communications in the region, that had been no mean feat.

"What exactly did happen?" Deep Blue asked. "Was it related to Brown's quantum computer scheme?"

"There's a lot I'm still trying to piece together, but I can assure you that Brown won't be a problem anymore."

There was a brief silence on the line, then the other man said simply: "Understood. Hold on." Deep Blue's muffled voice could be heard speaking to someone else for a moment. Then he came back on the line. "Lew is here. Has some intel you might find interesting. I'm putting you on speaker."

The phone crackled and then Aleman spoke. "Can you hear me?"

"Loud and clear," King said.

"I've been looking into Pradesh and it turns out even the mighty Shiva's security—and his bank—can't keep me out. He received several payments from Jovian Technologies, who it turns out, also designed the quantum phones for Brown. The root of Jovian is Jove, better known as Zeus, father of Hercules. Its speculation, but we all know how Alexander likes to name things, including himself, for the ancient Greek myths, many of which he created."

"Carutius," King said. "That's what he was calling himself this time. The same name he used when he married Acca Larentia, before the formation of Rome on the land he owned." The idea that Alexander owned the very land Rome was founded on never ceased to amaze King. They'd found an underground citadel belonging to Alexander, hidden beneath the ruins of the Roman Forum, but how much more of the city still belonged to him?

He turned his thoughts back to Pradesh. If the man was working for Jovian, did Alexander know the man was a cult member? *Of course he did.* Alexander wouldn't care if Pradesh threw himself into the singularity. What difference would the man's death make? As long as the man achieved his goal—to control the black hole somehow. Maybe direct it's path. What Alexander didn't know was that the quantum phones would grant the black hole sentient thought and allow it to chose its own path. That's when things got away from him. So the lingering question was, "What did Alexander want with a black hole?"

"That, I can't tell you," Aleman said. "But he was definitely working behind the scenes on this thing."

King looked up as Sara came out of the bathroom, one towel wrapped around her torso, another turban-like on her head, and he flashed her a smile. Alexander and his motives could wait. The man's secrets wouldn't be uncovered by dwelling on them. "Oh, I did meet up with Sara and Fiona. They're fine."

"I had no idea that I'd be putting them in danger," Deep Blue said, guiltily.

"Actually, I appreciate the gesture. And now that Brainstorm is finally kaput and Alexander has disappeared again, I think that family vacation you proposed is definitely in order."

Deep Blue paused, and then said, "King, as much as it

pains me to have to say this..."

King tensed. If it had been anyone on the other end of the line, he'd have already hung up, but if Deep Blue needed him for something, it most likely couldn't wait. "What is it?"

"Can you pick up one of those ear hats? I think I'm going to make Rook wear one for a year when—if—when we find him."

King laughed, said he'd pick up a few for all the new recruits, and hung up the phone.

Sara leaned against him. "All quiet on the home front?"

"For now." King leaned over and kissed her forehead, then he left the suite's master bedroom and knocked lightly on the door to Fiona's bedroom. He eased the door open and found the girl nestled in a cocoon of blankets, a pillow covering her eyes.

"Fi," he called out. "Up and at'em, lazybones. Let's go see what kind of trouble we can get into today."

The pillow fell away as Fiona sat up, her eyes wide with apprehension. "You're kidding, right?"

King was taken aback by her response. Fiona's sense of humor had yet to make a full recovery.

"Of course I'm kidding, kiddo." He gave her gentle smile. "It's Disney World. What could possibly happen?"

ABOUT THE AUTHORS

JEREMY ROBINSON is the author of numerous novels including SECONDWORLD and PULSE, INSTINCT, and THRESHOLD, the first three books in his exciting Jack Sigler series, which is also the focus of and expanding series of co-authored novellas deemed the Chesspocalypse. Robinson also known as the #1 Amazon.com horror writer, Jeremy Bishop, author of THE SENTINEL and the controversial novel, TORMENT. His novels have been translated into ten languages. He lives in New Hampshire with his wife and three children.

Visit him on the web, here:
www.jeremyrobinsononline.com

SEAN ELLIS is the author of several novels. He is a veteran of Operation Enduring Freedom, and has a Bachelor of Science degree in Natural Resources Policy from Oregon State University. He lives in Arizona, where he divides his time between writing, adventure sports, and trying to figure out how to save the world.

Visit him on the web, here:
seanellisthrillers.webs.com

ALSO AVAILABLE

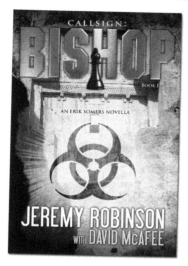

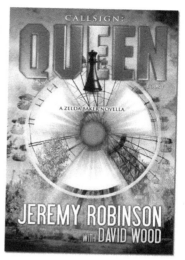

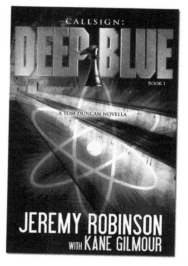